LEAP OF FAITH

When Carole falls in love she thinks William feels the same about her, but he's a man of faith. Carole is hesitant about expressing her true feelings to him. Then, when she resolves to tell him, his beautiful ex-girlfriend arrives and Carole decides to take time out. However, fate throws her handsome childhood hero Jason into her path. Carole chooses to follow her dreams, not knowing that one small step will lead her to take a leap of faith.

VALERIE HOLMES

LEAP OF FAITH

Complete and Unabridged

LINFORD
Leicester

First published in Great Britain in 2009

First Linford Edition
published 2010

British Library CIP Data

Holmes, Valerie.
    Leap of faith. - - (Linford romance library)
    1. Love stories.
    2. Large type books.
    I. Title II. Series
    823.9'2–dc22

    ISBN 978–1–84782–984–9

Published by
F. A. Thorpe (Publishing)
Anstey, Leicestershire

Set by Words & Graphics Ltd.
Anstey, Leicestershire
Printed and bound in Great Britain by
T. J. International Ltd., Padstow, Cornwall

This book is printed on acid-free paper

1

The first time Carole saw William he was wearing a long black cassock and standing on top of a ladder — not the most romantic of starts to any relationship but it was sort of typical for her life.

Nothing ever happened to her in life in the sequence of events that one would have naturally have expected it to — or at what would normally be considered the correct time.

However, from that first moment something inside her smiled every time she set eyes on him.

She had only popped into the church to ask if the bike outside belonged to someone in there. That is — someone other than the two teenage boys who had dropped it and fled when she had stumbled across them on the way to the shops.

It was a good excuse to actually cross the threshold of the church for the first time in years. Carole believed in God, as she always had done, but at that particular juncture she seemed to have drifted away from her faith — her roots.

Meanwhile she carried on, lost in the thick dark forest of life, not knowing which path to take to find her way out into the sunshine again.

That first sight was nearly six months ago, and now St Bede's was like a second home to her, and William — well he was more than a friend and confidant, but how much more she wasn't sure.

One question hounded her — did he feel the same way? Tonight, I shall find out! Carole was determined, for her own sanity's sake. If she had misjudged his friendship for something more than it was — well, Carole blanked the thought. Why cross bridges, as they say.

Carole pulled up outside George Brentley's house, just a couple of roads from the church. The rain swilled down

2

and her old Mini's windscreen wipers were going into warp speed as they struggled to cope with the downpour.

'Evening, Carole.' George's voice startled her as it interrupted her thoughts about William. Opening the passenger door as quickly as he could, George flopped on to the seat dripping water everywhere from his old mackintosh. 'You're a bit late. Can't have that William giving us the boot, can we, eh?' He dug her side with his wet elbow as he spoke just in case she had missed his latest pun on William's surname.

She grinned warmly at him. George cheered her up even on the wettest of days like today, because his jokes, particularly at the Revd William Boot's expense, were made with no malice intended. George was one of life's optimists.

Carole found his attitude quite inspiring compared with that of her sister, Judy, and her rather sombre husband, Graham. They had each other, young Tom, good jobs and a lovely house, yet they never seemed satisfied with their lot. Unlike George, who despite being widowed last year still found things about which he could smile. He pulled a large sack into the car and placed it in front of him on the already dampened floor.

Thank goodness I put the rubber mats back in Carole thought as she watched a pool of water collect by his feet as it ran off the bag. At five foot, he fitted in more easily than most people did into her small Mini.

'What've you got there, George?' Carole asked, as she waited for him to fasten his seat belt before signalling and pulling out into the road.

'Oh, just some bits and bobs to help fix the vicarage up. It needs quite a lot doing to it before the next Vicar arrives. Raymond asked me to do some jobs this coming week whilst he was at the Captain's Retreat.'

'The Captain's what?' Carole asked, as she struggled to see the road through the heavy rain.

'The Captain's Retreat is a small cabin down the coast road. Raymond went there the same week in February every year. He used to say it gave him back his perspective on life, away from parochial demands. He'd read up on all the form and take some Dick Francis books with him to keep him in the mood. He liked the horses did the old Vic.'

'Miss Simmons was ever so upset when I told her he wouldn't be coming this year. I put the card up in the hall to see if anyone else fancied a break, but it's such short notice and February isn't warm, is it? Well not for a holiday on our coast. Anyhow, as I was saying he meant to get the vicarage fixed up.'

'Well I suppose Reverend Tully did let the place run down a bit. I think he said he would decorate it throughout this summer. But then I suppose he didn't expect to die so soon.'

Carole could have kicked herself the moment she'd said the words. Most of the older parishioners had known the

5

Tully for years but Carole hadn't, and found his attitude on many subjects about as modern as a dinosaur except, it seemed, regarding gambling.

He had wanted to dictate to his flock, rather than nurture them like children — they were supposed to be God's children, weren't they?

'Well, if he didn't expect to die, then perhaps he of all people should've,' George replied matter-of-factly.

'Why?' Carole asked, as she drove into the church grounds negotiating the pot-holed drive round to the old vicarage, which nestled behind the church and the old hall. She parked as near to the door as she could.

'Well, lass, we all do. It's the only thing in life that's for certain, and we're always being reminded of the futility of mortality.' George pulled out the sack and Carole locked up her car feeling somewhat apprehensive at George's serious reply.

Had she hit on a raw nerve with George?

As if reading her thoughts he glanced back at her and beamed his brightest smile.

'Let's see what 'Sweet William's' got in store for us tonight.' Ever the gentleman he let Carole go in front of him.

Carole tried to ring the doorbell.

'No use doing that. It's one of the things that needs fixing,' George explained.

Carole knocked on the old green door and couldn't help noticing some paint flaking off next to the knocker. George was a retired builder; he could turn his hand to most jobs and had a keen sense of humour, which you either loved or loathed. Carole loved it because he was a 'doer' like herself.

The door opened and the hall light behind him silhouetted William's tall figure. Carole hesitated for a moment. Normally William was dressed in jeans and a shirt for these meetings, with or without the dog collar. Tonight, he had a new pair of dark brown casual slacks on, which matched perfectly with a smart Timberland shirt.

'Come on in out of the rain. It's an awful night.' William took the soggy sack from George. 'February is either too early for Santa impersonations, George — or too late, depending on your point of view,' William said placing it carefully down on the doormat.

'Don't you worry, Bill. This is a present you'll want, that's for sure. Some tools to do the jobs about the old place — like fixing that door bell.'

'What would I do without you, George?' William said fondly, as he hung George's coat up on the old hall-stand.

'You'd get people in that would do a poor job and present you with a big 'bill' — Bill?' George chuckled and went into the familiar living room.

William watched him with a broad smile spreading across his face replacing his initial wince. He turned to Carole who had deliberately hung back behind him.

'William, I wondered if we could . . . ' Carole hesitated as a familiar figure rushed up the hallway from the kitchen.

'Tea or coffee, Carole?' The voice of Mrs Emily Twiggs cut across her own words. 'Pardon?' Carole wasn't sure if she had snapped out her reply in a vexed voice. She hadn't meant to but, after all, speaking to William was important, more so than drinking a cup of tea.

'Tea please, Emily,' Carole said and forced herself to smile back.

'Right then, could you come and help me carry the other drinks through, Carole? I'm more than willing to make it but, I'm a bit more fragile than I used to be. My legs, you know.'

Emily did not wait for a reply; she was used to being obeyed. She had the air of an old schoolmarm about her. 'She, who must be obeyed,' George called her, out of her earshot of course. Reluctantly Carole followed her. Somehow, I must speak with William, she thought, but when we can be alone.

2

Carole took up her position in the kitchen with the aptly named Mrs Twiggs. She stood a full head height above Carole and at seventy her posture was as straight as a die.

The Revd Tully had always called her a will-o'-the-wisp because he thought she would bend if the wind blew her way. Carole saw her more as a fixed rod of iron. She looked delicate but there was an inner strength to Emily that Carole had always sensed.

Precariously, Carole carried the large wooden tray to the assembled group. It was a gloomy Victorian style room with old dark furniture, flock wallpaper and large deep red patterned rugs. The existing lighting from an assortment of fringed lamps was poor.

No one, as yet, had had the courage to change much, in respect for the late vicar, who hadn't liked light much. He had asked the very able Jean Howden to make heavy dark green curtains for it, with matching throws to go over the two old sofas, which faced each other at opposing edges of the faded Turkish rug.

Jean chatted animatedly to George as Carole offered her a drink. Surrounded by her handiwork, Jean was obviously quite at home. Her ample figure filled half of the sofa. She was as dishevelled in her long loose blouse and pleated polyester skirt, as Emily was smart in her maroon jersey dress, decorated with a tasteful gold snake brooch.

'That's great,' George gushed as he took his cup off the tray. He turned to Emily who was sitting in a stiff-backed dark wooden chair, as if leading the meeting. 'You make a lovely cuppa, Emily.'

Carole stifled a grin at Emily's restrained smile. She always seemed to be on edge when George was near. Perhaps it was his poor taste in jokes, which occasionally stretched to her name also.

'Hello. Sorry we're a bit late.' Sheila Downey's voice was as nervous as it always was.

'Not that it was our fault. Damn road-works! They're always closing some road or other.' Arthur Downey glanced at William who was standing behind them, and blushed slightly. 'Excuse the language, Vicar, but they have no consideration for road users like ourselves. They just dig the holes where they damn well please!'

'Well you're here now and that's what matters.' William took their wet coats and disappeared with them back into the hallway whilst the Downeys sat on the other sofa.

'Oh, a cup of tea, how lovely,' Sheila said, and smiled warmly at Carole.

'No sugar for me.' Arthur took the cup from the offered tray. He looked pointedly at Emily, as he would be chairing the meeting as treasurer and PCC member. If she was aware of him looking at her she gave no sign of it so he resigned himself to a seat on the sofa next to his wife.

'Well thank you for coming out on such an awful night as this.' William was standing next to Emily. He obviously had placed the hard chair there for himself and now glanced at the two sofas.

As if reading his thoughts Carole was standing at the opposite end and had also been wondering if she should squeeze in with George and Jean or sit with Sheila and the rather dour Arthur.

They both stepped towards George and almost collided. In joint muffled tones of apology Carole sat down next to George and William sat opposite her on the Downeys' sofa.

'Now we're all here, let us pray before we start.' William closed his eyes and looked down; each in the group followed his lead, except Carole who stared at him for a moment or so longer.

He normally looked lovely to her

with his wayward brown wavy hair and deep blue eyes. But today, dressed smartly — he looked perfect. She dared to wonder if her presence had something to do with it, then quickly rebuked herself for thinking such thoughts.

'Dear Lord, as we gather tonight for this meeting, be with us . . . ' William's mouth was moving and his words were flowing with the sincerity that always touched Carole. She held her head down and in her mind — in the same silent voice with which she had always talked to God, Carole said her own 'Thank yous'.

Thank you Lord, for William. Thank you for bringing me a true friend who I can trust, not like . . . well that's all in the past now. Thank you for . . .

'Amen.' William's voice cut through her prayer and she looked up, somewhat bleary eyed to see his face stare back at her and then he glanced around the group.

'Before we start, I just want to

explain that I have a visitor arriving during the course of the evening. She is an old friend of mine from university, who will be staying here for a few days. So I apologise if our meeting is disrupted in any way and would ask you to continue whilst I welcome her.'

There was a general mumbling of 'no problem', and a 'how lovely' from Sheila, but Carole said nothing. She looked in her bag as if searching for something.

What a presumptuous fool she'd been! He's dressed up for her — not me. They were at university together! He never said he didn't have a girlfriend. I never asked, I presumed. I want to leave! Carole could not explain the way she felt.

'Is this what you're looking for?' Emily held out a tissue discreetly as William continued talking about the state of the vicarage and asked for suggestions as to how it could be improved before a new vicar arrived.

'No. Thank you. I was looking for my

pen and paper.' Carole smiled a fixed unnatural smile. She proceeded to grunt and nod appropriately for the next half-hour to all suggestions made. She didn't want to agree, disagree or volunteer. She just wanted to leave. This was not like her usual enthusiastic manner but no one seemed to notice.

I'm supposed to be a Christian — I'm supposed to offer to help. God, why am I a fool? Why do I always want what is beyond my ability to have?

The meeting came to an abrupt halt as a car was heard in the drive shortly followed by a rapid but light knocking on the door. William stood up straight away. 'Excuse me.' He left swiftly and everyone tried to continue in conversation so as not to be seen to listen to the events in the hallway.

He's keen — eager even!

'Will!' The female's voice was filled with joy. Next there came muffled laughter and chatter, and the sound of a bag being put down on the stairs. Carole glanced at Arthur who was looking upwards, not for divine inspiration but in a display of displeasure at the frivolity coming from the hallway.

She could almost hear his thoughts. 'It would never have happened in Reverend Tully's day.' Moments later the door was opened and William introduced his friend.

'This is Susan.' William was followed into the room by a vision of long-legged, blonde haired beauty wearing jeans and a figure-hugging top.

That's it. I stand no chance, thought Carole.

Everyone gave her a warm welcome, except for Carole who sat quietly, letting others do the pleasantries.

'Would you like a hot drink? Tea? Coffee?' Carole suddenly realised how she could be friendly and escape briefly to the kitchen.

'Water would do fine. I don't drink caffeine; it's bad for my skin.'

Carole nodded and made a beeline for the doorway to escape from her worst nightmare — the dream on legs that had an unblemished skin, who Carole did not doubt was as beautiful on the inside as she was on the outside. Or else why would someone as genuine as William, like her?

Carole carried the glass of water towards the hall, only to come face to face with William.

'Carole was there something you wanted to say to me earlier?'

Carole's mouth dropped open. If only he'd said that when she arrived she would have told him exactly what she wanted him for. 'Yes, but it's not important. I'll catch you when you're not so busy.'

Behind him Susan loitered by the bottom of the stairway. She was running her fingers carefully through her long hair, finger drying it. Carole could not help herself but admire anyone who could look as good when wet as they did when dry.

Carole handed her the glass of water and rejoined the meeting. It was agreed to completely change the vicarage to bring it into this century, tastefully and of course cheaply. In church life there was never any money for anything and Arthur Downey was the Treasurer.

'Well you can go to the second hand thrift shops for bits of furniture, or to look for bargains in the sales.' Arthur was penny pinching on everything. 'The furniture that is here is perfectly good enough. It just needs a bit of work on it.'

'Restaining perhaps?' George couldn't wait to get his hands on it and do a makeover. 'We can get some of the youngsters helping with the redecorating and then lighten the place up a bit.'

'Now there's a depressing thought!' Arthur was getting on to one of his favourite bandwagons.

William returned just in time for the two to regain the Christian spirit of working together. Carole sat quietly; for once she did not volunteer for anything. The vicarage was now the last place she wanted to be.

'Well if that's agreed, then we'll call it

a day. Thank you for coming.'

Carole was the first to stand up before anyone, and fetched George his coat from the hall. The rain had subsided. She said a quick 'Bye' to everyone and climbed into her car only to realise she had left her bag by the end of the sofa.

Blast! Now I have to go back in and everyone has left.

'George, I forgot my bag'. She handed him the key to the Mini and ran back to the front door. Forgetting, she rang the silent bell. Damn! She knocked hard but still there was no answer.

Opening the side gate, she had no choice but to run around to the kitchen door. It was raining again so she hurried. The light was on; she peered through the window between the leaded lights and could see two figures. William and Susan.

She was about to knock when Susan wrapped her arms around William and planted a kiss firmly on his lips. Carole saw the two of them embrace and stood back from the window, rain soaking her hair that she knew would look like rats' tails — not like Susan's had. Carole retraced her steps.

'Can't you make him hear you?' George was standing at the front by the door waiting for her in the shelter of the porch.

Crumbs, he mustn't see them! William should think of his position.

'No, George, I couldn't.'

'Well I will!' He turned and pounded on the front door. Moments later, William rushed to open it.

'No need to panic, Bill.' George looked at William's surprised face. 'Young Carole forgot her bag and couldn't get you to hear her knock. I told you I should fix that bell for you.'

William looked flustered and George chuckled as though it was his remonstration that had caught William off guard.

'Don't worry, Bill. I'll sort it out tomorrow.'

Carole rushed into the living room and tried not to drip too much and was back out of the door in a second. She thought she caught a glimpse of Susan's figure in the kitchen doorway but did not turn to acknowledge her presence.

As she passed by William she avoided looking at him but muttered her apologies instead then beat a hasty retreat to her car.

'There now. Sometimes a bit of brute force gets results,' George informed her, and then chatted enthusiastically about the work he would undertake to transform the old vicarage. Carole couldn't wait for him to get out of the car so she could drive off and be on her own.

She felt like a fool. How could I have imagined he actually cared for me? It's his job to care for everyone. How desperate am I? How could I mistake caring for loving? What a fool I am. A thirty-six-year-old one at that. God — how could a love which felt so right be so misplaced? Carole went on home alone.

3

Don't think about him! Carole told herself for what seemed like the millionth time that morning. She stretched and put her arms outside the quilt to test the temperature. The heating hadn't come on yet, which meant it had to be before six a.m.

Carole couldn't stand it any more — if her brain wouldn't sleep then it was no good confining her body to the bed. Quietly, she lifted her dressing gown from the hook by the bed and tiptoed out of her room, being careful not to wake her nephew, young Tom.

Three-year-olds sleep so soundly, she thought as she passed the open door of his adjoining room. Originally the au-pair had slept there, but that hadn't worked out so somehow Carole had stepped into the role.

In the kitchen Carole put on the

kettle and made herself a cup of tea. A cure for all ills — a nice cup of tea! She sat down at the large oak table and picked up one of Judy's magazines. The words on the front page leapt out at her, **Take control of your life — now!**

Carole sipped her tea and nestled herself into her favourite chair by the radiator, and read: 'What do you want out of life? Do you know who you really are? Do you feel you could do more than you are?'

Carole laughed and was going to turn the page when she saw the questionnaire. In her mind she answered the questions and totted up her score. Hey! I've scored quite high. Feeling quite pleased with herself she eagerly read on.

'It's time you redefined your goals in life. Your score indicates that you are feeling low self-esteem and have not fulfilled your ambitions. Take some time out — NOW. Write down what you want out of your life. Then write down what you already have and then decide on ten steps that you can take to bridge the gap. It's your life so take control of it today.'

Crikey! She thought, there's nothing like reading something positive to cheer yourself up, and that was nothing like anything positive. Or was it? Carole fiddled with the handle of the cup and sighed, I know I exist but am I really alive?

'You're an early bird this morning. What's wrong, is Tom OK?' A concerned look crossed Judy's immaculately made-up face.

'Don't worry, he's fine. I just couldn't sleep.' Carole watched her younger sister reach for her morning yoghurt from the fridge and make herself a cup of lemon tea.

She was a trim size eight and always smart. Carole waited for her to ask if she was OK. But she was disappointed. Judy was getting ready for work and nothing stopped her concentration on her preparation.

'Carole, would you be a love and take

Tom to the library this morning and then on to Mrs Henderson's for eleven?'

Carole glanced down at the magazine. Take control of your life! The words stood out at her, she was supposed to be free today. 'No sorry, I can't.'

'Thanks, Graham's got a golf match and . . . what did you say?'

'I said, no, sorry, Judy, but I can't.'

Judy looked at her in disbelief. 'Why ever not? It's Saturday morning. You weren't going anywhere.'

'I don't usually, that's true, but I can't this Saturday because today I am. I need some time out.' Carole felt her confidence growing. She normally fitted in but today she wanted some space to think.

'Time out for what?' Judy asked, as she glanced at her wristwatch, cheeks flushed, without waiting for Carole to reply. 'You'll have to sort it out with Graham or I'll be late. He will not be pleased, Carole.'

Carole shrugged and thought, tough! So before Graham arrived Carole dressed and grabbed the magazine and a few things from the kitchen to put into her rucksack. She left a note for Graham relaying Judy's instructions and left.

Today I'm living for me! Carole took her car to the church car park and borrowed William's bike from the old hall. She knew it was his day off and he wouldn't be going anywhere on it with Susan in tow. Parking in town on a Saturday was an expensive business. This way she would be free to go where the will took her with the wind in her hair.

★ ★ ★

Five lonely hours later she was sitting on the end of a pier in February, drawing. Carole looked fondly down at her old sketchbook. Like an old friend she was glad she had it. Drawing usually took her mind off her problems.

I'm here to forget William, Judy, and even young Tom, lovely as he is. Carole tried to reflect on herself and her own future, whilst she still had enough of her life left to make one of her own, and not dwell on the past. I've got to change. The more she reprimanded herself for being as she was, the more defeatist she became.

If she could only afford to rent that cabin, the *Captain's Retreat* for the week, Carole was sure that would be long enough for her to sort herself, and her life out. Then she remembered some of her mum's words of wisdom — 'No one can go forward if they are constantly looking backwards.' Carole knew it was true, but feeling retrospectively dismal was becoming habitual behaviour.

Carole looked at the pencil and sketchbook on her lap. The pencil was half its original length; the best and newest half had been used up. Carole reflected on the well-worn bit that was left.

That was how she felt; the best part of her life, her youth, had vanished in taking care of others. First her mother, then Judy and now Tom by default. She had the well worn half left.

Stop it! Her inner voice saved her from more gloomy thoughts and she shoved her pad into her bag, taking great care to find a safe place for her pencil. I will change!

Swinging her rucksack on to her back she looked around at the open expanse of the sea. Walking over to the railings at the very end of the pier, she gazed down at the swirling water beneath as it moved menacingly around the pylons. It was dark, moody and yet, wonderful.

Carole closed her eyes and lifted her head high. The salty air caressed her face, as each gust of wind gathered in strength and intensity. She smiled remembering the strong winds that had nearly knocked her off her feet as she ran along the beach of her childhood. There, the wind blew in gales along the North East Coast, well if not all the time, most of it, or that is how it had seemed in her memory.

If only the wind could blow all my troubles away. Most of the population of Britain would be lined up along the coastline if it could. Carole grinned at the image in her mind, then as she opened her eyes she saw that she was not alone. A tall figure in an exquisite leather jacket was leaning against the pier railings, almost hidden behind the small lifeboat house on the end of the pier.

Carole recognised him instantly. His casual trousers and shoes were equally well made. She could tell they were designer clothes, even if she had no idea whose labels would be attached to them. She had never needed to know such things. He was rubbing his hand through his thick collar length hair, which still held some of its original raven colouring, amongst the more silvery tones.

Carole tried not to stare at him; she glanced around the end of the pier. A family was running past the small restaurant buildings to catch the train that would take them back down the mile of its length. As the wind strengthened, most sane people had returned. February was not a busy month in the life of a pier, unless it was the half term holidays; then, freezing or not, it swarmed with well-wrapped children wanting out of season ice cream, slush, doughnuts or candyfloss.

She moved to within a few yards of where he was standing. At first he didn't seem to be aware of her presence. The child she once was quivered inside her. A rush of excitement caused her to shake. It's Jason Forbes — I can't believe my luck!

Carole remembered Thursday nights, cycling from school desperate to be home for four o'clock in order to see her hero. There were no videos in those days. You had to be there on time to see a programme. She must have been fourteen, nearly twenty-two years ago!

No wonder the face of her hero had

dropped slightly, creases had formed on the surface of his skin, but he still had a strong well-defined jaw line. But there was no mistaking it was him. He turned and looked at her. He still had penetrating, to die for, deep brown eyes.

Carole was holding on to the railings, firmly balanced against the wind and stopping her legs from buckling under her with excitement. How had she managed to find her childhood hero, here — a mile out to sea, on the end of a pier? Absurdly, it all seemed like an adolescent dream.

It was strange remembering herself as a fourteen-year-old. Those days she'd felt alive, and full of dreams of becoming an actress and of meeting him. But they were only empty dreams, as useless to her as asking her what she wanted to do when she left school.

What was the point of wishing she could be free to carry on schooling, go through university or drama school and venturing out into the world to use her love of art and words. Pointless when you have an ill mother and young sister to care for. It wasn't their fault, but she had been needed — trapped. Yet now, all these years later he was here. Thank you God for this one magical moment. Please let it last.

'Is there nowhere I can escape and be alone?' His voice was harsh and abrupt. It jolted her from her thoughts, but she tried hard not to show it.

'Pardon?' Carole said politely, and smiled at him. He looked the other way. Had she been dismissed? She felt foolish, again, but something about his manner made her want to persevere. Not the awe-struck child trapped inside her, but the woman who didn't like his attitude and was fed up with being taken for granted.

She had spent the last twenty years with a growing sense of nothingness, the invisible, affable Carole, reliable, hardworking daughter and then sister — or was she just a mug? She had tried to do her Christian duty by her family but where had it got her?

She grinned as she always did when she had allowed herself a moment of self-pity — at the end of a pier, in February, that's where. Carole felt so totally happy in the knowledge that this time, though, she wasn't alone.

'Looks like a downpour.' Carole gestured to the train. 'That was the last one of the day.'

'So?' he snapped at her rather abruptly.

'So, I thought you might like to know, as it's a long walk back.' Carole smiled broadly back at him, determined that she would not let his manner appear to unnerve her even if her knees felt very shaky.

Her hero had never snapped at anyone when he was on TV. He had climbed the rigging, fought pirates and was always chivalrous to maidens in distress. Carole was amazed that she should feel that same rush of excitement all these years later. For the first time in what seemed like an age the dreamer she had once been was being rekindled; she felt a growing sense of adventure rise within her.

Carole had no idea why he wanted to be alone. Perhaps he wanted to escape from something too.

'The end of a pier isn't really a good place to escape.' She looked directly at him, brave, bold and determined not to waver in her stare. His eyes focused on her, so she pointed down to the sea. 'There are only two ways to escape — down there, which is cold and rather wet, or back the way you came.' Carole gestured along the pier then turned her face back to his, meeting his gaze again.

He considered her for a moment. She was only five feet three inches tall so he had to look down at her; she was used to people doing that but he seemed to do it with a patronising air about him.

'Are you a reporter — did you follow me here?'

Carole laughed out loud. 'Me — a reporter! Why ever would I follow you?'

She saw him straighten up, obviously taken aback. He let go of the railings and gestured openly with his hands.

'I'm Jason Forbes!' he exclaimed. There was a note of arrogance in his voice, which grated on Carole. She responded instantly, deciding to plead ignorance of any knowledge of him.

'Hi.' Carole held out her hand to him. 'I'm glad to meet you, Mr Ford.'

'Jason Forbes,' he repeated looking at her quizzically.

'Sorry. Well the wind's getting up and bringing that storm ever nearer, so I'll be making my way back to town. Nice to meet you.'

Carole started to walk back down the pier's length. She couldn't believe she had just walked away from the man who had been perfect in the eyes of the schoolchild she had once been. She leaned into the wind as she left the shelter of the buildings and headed back along the open pier. At least there were shelters with seats where she could take cover if the heavens opened.

A few minutes later she had to dive into one of the recently painted marine blue shelters. The storm had arrived. The rain was so heavy it reminded her of the monsoon rain they had shown on a holiday programme of Malaysia.

Carole was just deciding their rain must be a damn sight warmer than this was, when Jason dashed in, cursing, and wildly brushing his hair frantically with his hands as if trying to disperse the rain that had already flattened it. Her hero had never bothered about his hair when on the decks in a storm. Then it had been long and tied back into a little ponytail at the nape of his neck.

Rummaging around in her rucksack for something to do, Carole found a pack of polo mints. She put one in her mouth and offered the packet to Jason. 'Would you like one?'

He gave her that *how dare you speak to me* look again, so she shrugged her shoulders and withdrew her offending mints.

'Yes.' He stopped fingering his hair and seemed to plump his hands into his coat pockets as if giving it up as a bad job. 'I mean, thank you, I'd love a mint.' He held out a hand towards her.

Carole moved a little nearer so that she could hand him the packet. He smiled and she felt herself flutter again. Compose yourself, you're a grown woman, not a lovesick girl. She looked the opposite way peering up at the sky.

'If it doesn't ease we'll just have to make a run for it,' Carole said and could have kicked herself for being so blatantly British and talking about the weather. He had been the man of her dreams and she was offering him polo mints and talking to him about rain! At least she hadn't given William a thought for at least half-an-hour.

'What are you then if you're not a reporter?' he asked her whilst shoving his hands deeply into his jacket pockets again. Carole had noticed his suntan, which did not come from a British seaside resort in February.

'That's an odd question,' Carole remarked.

'Why?' She had his attention; he genuinely wanted to know.

'Most people's first question would be who are you, not what are you.' Carole watched a broad grin cross his face. Now that's more like my hero, she thought. 'Why should I be a reporter anyway?' She couldn't resist the challenge of acting her part out. Could she fool him, convince a professional actor with her own part, and not give her feelings of excitement away?

'I'm Jason Forbes.' He stared at her. 'The actor.'

'Oh! Sorry.' Carole popped a mint into her mouth before continuing. 'I don't get to the pictures much, you'll have to excuse me.' She smiled apologetically, whilst she tried with all her might to control herself and remain composed. 'I'm Carole Kirkpatrick, a . . . ' Carole thought 'MUG' would fit but then remembered her sketchbook, 'artist — well an illustrator to be more precise.'

'You won't see me at the 'pictures'. I work on TV and stage mainly.' He looked down at her then suddenly stood up and swore at the rain. 'Damn! This country and its miserable weather!'

'Is it really the weather you're cursing?' Carole watched him turn around slowly and look at her. Distrust was blatant across his face.

'You are very presumptive, Ms Kirkpatrick.'

'Perhaps, but usually it can be expected to be pretty miserable in February. This isn't the best place to come to top up your suntan. So unless you love the fresh salty air of the sea, then there's usually another reason.'

He leaned against the inside of the shelter. 'Why did you come here then? Do you have a particular liking for salty air?'

Carole laughed. 'OK, I'll come clean. I wanted to get away.'

'From what?' he asked.

'Me, my life, I suppose. Ties and responsibilities.'

He sat back down and casually crossed his legs. 'The husband and kids getting too much for you, are they?'

'Now who's being presumptuous? There is no husband and kids. So why are you here?'

'It's easing. Nice to meet you.' He walked off down the pier.

Carole followed. She saw him pass the next shelter half way down the pier's length when the monsoon began again. She had just made it into the shelter and huddled herself up on the seat when he dived back in.

She opened her rucksack and found what she was searching for. 'Here,' she said, holding out a small hand towel to him. His hands were ruffling his soaking hair again.

'Do you always carry one with you?' he asked as he took it and towel dried his hair.

'Usually, when I have my rucksack

with me. I carry it for Thomas — he can get so messy at times.'

'Thomas?'

'My three-year-old nephew. I look after him while my sister's at work. Well I do sometimes, anyway.' She took the wet towel back from him and put it in a plastic carrier bag that she had also pulled out of her rucksack. 'Would you like a coffee?'

'What?' he was grinning at her. His face lit up with genuine humour as she produced two small flasks, a plastic spoon and a couple of sachets of sugar. 'Were you a Girl Guide or something?'

'No. Never went to anything like that, but I like a hot drink on a cold day.' Carole took the two white plastic cups off the flasks and carefully placed them on the wooden plank of the seat. She pointed to the red flask first and asked, 'Black or . . . ?' pointing to the blue flask, 'Latte or . . . ?' and reached into the outside pocket of her rucksack and produced a small bottle, 'Gaelic?'

'Gaelic, thanks.' He watched as she

carefully made up the two drinks and handed him one.

'Sorry about the plastic cups but beggars can't be choosers, I suppose.'

'There's a first time for everything,' Jason replied as he sipped the drink suspiciously at first but then gulped it down with obvious approval.

'So why are you here?' Carole felt perfectly at liberty to ask him seeing as he had asked her and was now happily enjoying her coffee — plastic cup or not.

'You'd go to the press.' Jason didn't even look at her. It was just a statement of fact to him.

'You really know how to trust a person, don't you?' Carole watched him drink the end of his coffee and put the cup down next to her.

'When you've been in the acting profession as long as I have you learn to be discerning about who you confide in.' He stood up and leaned against the shelter, staring out at the rain.

'Sounds like a lonely life to me.

Anyway, I'm different. I trust people until they prove to me that they are not deserving of it.' She carefully packed up her things.

'Then you must frequently be let down and hurt.' He was watching her, but not mocking or grinning. He seemed to be looking for a genuine reaction to his statement.

'True,' Carole answered as she swung her bag on to her back. 'But at least I'm not a cynic. Race you to the next shelter.' Without waiting she ran as a brief respite in the rain brought a momentary flash of sunshine.

When Carole was ten yards off the final shelter she was surprised to hear Jason's footsteps chasing her. Like two children they raced each other and both collapsed on the bench together laughing.

'I can't believe I just did that,' he said, as he regained his composure. 'You are different, certainly different to Melissa.' His smile vanished instantly and he sat upright gritting his teeth.

'Is she your wife?' Carole asked, but couldn't help hoping that he wasn't married. It was an absurd hope. She knew she didn't stand a chance with such a celebrity as Jason. He was one of life's high flyers.

She was down to earth. Plain and spinster material. Even William with his kind heart and hard work was too good for the likes of her. Yet, she hoped against hope that Jason was still free and uncomplicated.

'Heavens no. Well I hoped she would be, but she had other ideas.' He looked at her. 'I proposed, and she went off with a guitarist half my age.'

Carole could see the bitterness in his eyes, and the hurt. 'How old is Melissa?'

'Twenty-six.'

'Ah!' Carole stood up ready to walk the last part of the pier back to the seafront.

'What's the 'ah' meant to mean?' He was standing behind her.

'I suppose she may have felt too

young to settle down.' She did not look at him as she spoke. Carole did not mean to be offensive, but if she was young again and free, the last thing she would want is to be tied down.

'Oh, do you now. Do you also presume that I am too old for her?'

His face was flushed and he stood with his hands clenched at his side. For a moment she thought of Thomas.

'You are one messed up individual. I think for myself actually. Goodbye, Mr Forbes.'

Carole stepped out, walking in the sunshine along the sodden pier boards. It was only moments before she felt him following behind her and smelt his musk again.

'I didn't mean to be insulting. We're from different worlds. That's all. I appreciate your kindness . . . the coffee, but I need time on my own to think. Oh no!'

Carole looked up to see him staring at a figure walking along the seafront. It was a young man, carrying a bag and a camera.

'If he sees me he'll have a feature for sure. *Down and out actor's play collapses as his girl runs off with a guitarist*. Blast!'

Carole stopped and rummaged in her rucksack pulling out a large blue cagoule. 'Here, put this on.' She helped him pull it over his jacket and put the hood up.

'It's gross!' he exclaimed.

'Who cares, it's big enough to cover me and my rucksack when I'm on my bike. If you really want to escape, then I'll help you.'

She linked arms with him and walked to the pier's small train station where she unlocked the old bike. 'Climb on the back.'

'You're joking, aren't you?'

'Not if you want to avoid him.' Carole nodded at the figure that was walking along the path towards them, staring into each shop that he passed.

'OK, OK.' Jason held the handlebars. 'You sit on the seat and I'll drive — pedal. Just tell me where to go.'

'Great, I mean, turn left!' Heaven! Carole held his waist firmly and hung on tight as he pushed the bike off into the road. Carole could have cried tears of joy.

4

'Beep, Beep, Beep' — William rolled over and firmly hit his alarm clock. Then he groaned as the realisation that it was his day off sank in. 'Oh, I should've switched it off.' Gazing up at the ceiling, studying the old artex, he pondered, Should I get up? Just ten more minutes then I'll see if Sue's stirred yet.

William was pleased to see his friend again. She reminded him of days that had been filled with laziness and carefree fun, unlike those he served in today. The Revd Tully's death had been unfortunate in many ways. It had forced William into taking on much more of the administration of the parish than he felt comfortable with.

Although the PCC were responsible for the transition between priests, he was obviously expected to do more duties to help. William wanted to be more involved with people, doing God's real work, dispensing with protocol and meetings. The phone ringing cut across his thoughts. It's my day off! When the answer-phone did not come on he reluctantly left his bed.

Passing the door of the spare bedroom he could see Susan draped across her bed. Even when asleep, she's still beautiful. William remembered the previous night's kiss. It brought back many pleasant, if not sinful, memories. The phone persisted so he jumped down the last few stairs and picked up the receiver.

'Hello, William speaking.' He slumped down on to the bottom step as he saw the clock in the hall showing a time of seven fifty-five.

'William,' the faint voice of a female whispered at the other end of the phone.

'Yes, who is it?' William asked as his senses returned to him.

'Emily Twiggs . . . I thought you weren't there.'

'Emily. I was in bed. Today's my day off and I'm taking my friend out and . . . '

'William I need you, I'm not well. Could you come round please?'

'What's wrong, Emily? Have you called a doctor?'

'Yes, it's my chest . . . I need you to come . . . Please.' Emily's voice sounded weak and so fragile.

William glanced up the stairs towards the spare room. Perhaps if I'm quick I'll be back in time to take Sue out. 'OK Emily I'll be round within the hour.' William replaced the receiver to the hushed tones of Emily's grateful voice.

By the time he'd changed, grabbed a drink and left an apologetic note for Sue, asking her to wait for his call, it was nearly nine. He would have rushed but Emily had done this once before and although she had looked pale and fragile, after a hot drink she seemed fine.

The Revd Tully called her a hypochondriac, but William was not so sure.

In any case the fear he sensed in her was genuine, even if the illness wasn't. William took the car keys out with him then remembered he had to collect it from the garage as it had not passed its MOT and had needed some work doing on it. So instead, he picked up his keys for the hall. He'd cycle there. He looked ominously at the sky. Then he saw Carole's car parked behind the church. Great, she'll give me a lift.

William walked around to the front of the church only to be greeted by Arthur Downey's solemn face.

'Oh, hello Arthur, I was looking for Carole; her car's outside.'

'Well she's not in here. William, I want to talk to you about the arrangements for Sunday's services. I'm not sure having the children in . . . '

'Arthur, I'm sorry to interrupt but I'm in a fix. I need to get to Emily Twiggs; she's not well and it's my day off and . . . '

'When one of your flock's sick, a vicar has no day off! Your time is God's time.'

William was finding his temper rising as he looked at Arthur, but had no time to debate the point. 'Excuse me, Arthur, I must get my bike. My car's in the garage.' Without waiting for Arthur's reply he opened the hall door only to find an empty space where his bike usually stood. 'Blast it!'

'Humph!' Arthur was standing behind William.

'My bike's gone!' William locked up the hall again. 'Arthur, could you give me a lift to Emily's?'

'Well, I was about to suggest it when you came over here. Yes, and it will give me a chance to talk about you involving all these children and teenagers in everything. I told you they were a bunch of thieving . . . well anyway. The door's open.'

Arthur started the engine with what William could see was great pride. William climbed into the BMW and by the time they pulled up outside Emily's house William had heard the phrase, 'In Revd Tully's day, this would never have been allowed,' at least three times.

With his blood pressure rising he thanked Arthur and left him to drive off as he knocked on Emily's door. As he hit it, it opened slightly. 'Emily,' William called as he made his way into the small terraced house.

'I'm here.' Her voice seemed stronger than it had been on the phone. A sudden guilty feeling flowed over him as he heard it. It was now half-past nine. He had taken longer to arrive than he had anticipated with not having his own transport.

Peeping around the frosted glass door into her living room he saw her figure sitting on her settee propped up with pillows behind her and her feet up on the cushions. Usually Emily was immaculately turned out, but today she wore a long flowery cotton night-dress, with a white crocheted shawl around her shoulders. Her hair had not been brushed, and she looked quite pale.

'You're not supposed to look shocked when you see people who are not at their best, Vicar.' Emily's lips turned up in a smile as she spoke.

'You are quite right, Emily, it's just I've only seen you well groomed, should we say?'

'We can if you like. I think that was the doctor, William.'

'What was?' William had not heard anything, then the door bell rang. His surprised expression brought more of a faint smile to Emily's face.

'That is.'

William let the doctor in. He was a locum and quite young. Efficient nonetheless.

'Angina,' he declared. 'We need to check you out though. Do you have any transport?' The doctor looked at William.

'I'm afraid not.'

'Would you be able to stay with her until the ambulance arrives?'

'Will it be long?' William asked trying not to make eye contact with Emily as a twinge of guilt swept through him. The doctor shrugged and he realised it was one of those how long is a piece of string questions. William had suddenly wanted to say no, and go back to see Susan, but he couldn't — he was needed. 'Of course I'll stay.'

The relief on Emily's face told William he had made the right choice.

With careful instructions on where he would find her small bag, ready packed for such an event, William was sent upstairs to her bedroom. He'd always imagined her living in a dreary Victorian type of house, rather like the vicarage, but in stark contrast to this, her bedroom was decorated in cream and white. It was light, airy and had quite modern built in units. A large teddy bear sat opposite the bed in its own armchair.

There were fresh flowers on the side table, lovely peach roses from the garden. A line of books filled a shelf to the side of the window. All of them were children's classics, such as the Chronicles of Narnia, Alice in Wonderland, and a full set of Disney books alongside the works of Tolkien. William realised he was taking too long and returned swiftly to the living room.

'This one?' he asked, as he held out a small tapestry weekend bag. As he did, he saw an address label still tied to it marked Disneyland Paris.

'Yes, thank you.' Emily looked at him. 'You're speechless, which is quite an achievement for a preacher man.'

'You tease me, Emily Twiggs.' William sat on the edge of the sofa next to her. 'So how long have you been a closet child?'

'Since I was a child. I never had the things I really wanted when I was younger. My parents were busy trying to provide food for us. Then my dear husband was very adult about everything. Now, as a widow, no one cares what the crazy old woman does, so I humour my childhood whims.'

'You are far from crazy. How did you know the doctor was here? I have excellent hearing and I didn't hear a thing?' William asked and the doorbell rang again.

'That's the ambulance, William. Phone your friend whilst they sort me out.'

William looked at his watch, it was nearly ten o'clock.

'William,' Emily said as the ambulanceman went for the stretcher, 'thank you for coming.'

He nodded and quickly phoned his own telephone number. To his surprise instead of hearing his own voice on the answer phone he heard a message from Susan. 'Darling, I'll be at The Grape Vine at twelve-thirty, meet me there for lunch.'

He grinned to himself at her resourcefulness but hoped nobody else had phoned him today, particularly Arthur Downey.

The ambulance men were very efficient. Emily was very tense. He held her hand and sat quietly by her side as she was taken into a room waiting for an ECG to be done. An hour and a half later she had been seen by a doctor who gave her a prescription and told her to make a further appointment with her

GP. They arrived back home in a taxi amidst pouring rain.

'Can you wait for my friend to come back to the car and take him back to the vicarage?'

'Yes, darlin',' the driver responded and opened the door, whilst William swept Emily's light frame up into his arms and carried her to her front door.

'William, you've quite swept me off my feet,' Emily joked as they reached her door.

'You're beginning to sound like George,' William commented as he put her down on her doorstep.

'Please, no, anything but that.' She grinned sheepishly. 'Go and enjoy your lunch with your friend.'

'I may miss her; she is not the most patient of people,' William explained as he put the collar up on his jacket against the rain.

'No, but you are — and that is a precious gift. She'll still be there. Enjoy your lunch and thank you for taking the time to help an old lady find a fast track through the NHS.'

'Pardon?' William looked back at her as he stepped up the path.

'Well now, do you think they dared to leave me in a corridor, waiting hours, with you there?' She grinned and waved goodbye as she shut the door.

William shook his head as he climbed back into the taxi. He put his hand in his pocket and found a ten pound note. He looked back to the house as the taxi drove off. How or when she had put the note there he did not know but she surely intended to pay for the taxi. William was hugely relieved as he had come out without any money in the chaos of the morning.

William had just time to change and get his old golf umbrella out of the wardrobe before making his way to meet Susan.

'Hi.' He tried to sound light, non-stressed and as relaxed as possible.

She turned and lifted her lips to his then withdrew them quickly. 'Do you have to wear that all the time?' Susan pointed to his dog collar.

Quickly William removed it and was instantly rewarded by a very warm embrace and passionate kiss on the lips.

'You're blushing.' She sat back down at their table. 'What have they done to you, Will?'

'Have you ordered?' William asked as he propped his brolly in a suitable corner.

'No. I thought I had better find out if you intended to come first.'

'Sorry, Sue. Emily Twiggs is an old lady who has a heart condition.'

'Yes. She calls and you run. Aren't you allowed any time off?' Sue asked as she looked up at him with her pale blue eyes and blonde hair framing her face.

He saw the same beauty and felt the same desire as if it was only yesterday that they had been together.

'Yes, today is my day off, but it's difficult. I swore before God to minister to the sick and prepare the dying for death; besides, the last Reverend had a heart attack and died.'

'Overworked, no doubt.' Sue grinned impishly.

'You're incorrigible.' William smiled back at her, even though a voice deep within his conscience told him he shouldn't. You're playing with fire, William, don't let yourself get burned!

'True, but that was what you loved about me once.' She turned to the waiter as they ordered. William watched the young man discreetly take in every contour of her figure hugging tee shirt as he wrote the order down. Putty in her hands — they all are. So was I.

'William, do you remember our visit to Paris?' Sue asked innocently as she sipped a glass of red wine.

'Of course I do.' William watched her running her finger around the edge of her glass.

'Why don't we visit again — for old times' sake?'

'For one reason, I can't. I've a parish to help run and besides . . . ' he sipped his lager, stopping mid conversation in an embarrassed pause.

'Besides what?' Susan placed her hand over his on the table and he felt the old passions rise within him.

How I remember Paris — if only . . . 'Besides which I can't afford it. A curate's salary is only a fraction of my old one. Here's our order.'

Susan turned her face from the frown, which had shadowed it as William had rebuffed her idea, to smile charmingly at the waiter as he placed their food on the table and left them to eat.

'I'll pay. Find a locum or whatever to cover you for a few days. Kick up your heels again and have some fun.' Susan started to eat her salad, bereft of mayonnaise or dressings that could endanger her figure.

'It's not that simple, as well you know. So stop teasing me and enjoy our time together.' William tucked into his ploughman's.

'OK. I'll not give up so easily though. I bought you something.' Susan put her hand in one of the many carrier bags, which she had leant against the wall. She pulled out a designer suit.

'Sue! You can't go spending that kind of money on me. I can't possibly give you any such gift in return. You'd better take it back. Thanks all the same.' William's face flushed as he remembered the days when she had been on a pittance and he had bought her such gifts with ease.

'Yes you will. You have to.' She beamed at him.

'Why?'

'Because to reject a gift because it hurts your pride is a sin. Besides, if I remember correctly from the lovely convent institution that I frequented as a child, you have to give. It's better than receiving is it not?'

'Yes, precisely my point!' William stressed his words.

'Then for me to give, you have to receive — humility, Will.'

'Thank you!' William said the word through an exaggerated gesture of gritting his teeth. They both laughed.

'So what did you get yourself or, should I say how many outfits did you buy?'

'Three,' Sue replied as she rummaged in the bottom of her bag. 'And this, it's the very latest in anti-wrinkle creams.'

'But you don't have any wrinkles,' William replied mockingly.

'Proves it works then,' Sue declared, and then pointed her finger at him. 'And don't lecture me about vanity, OK?'

'Let's call a truce, and accept each other for what we are.' William raised his glass and they both drank a toast to friendship and relaxed into the easy companionship they had once shared.

By the time they returned to the vicarage it was nearly five o'clock. They had both got thoroughly wet as they walked to pick up William's old Renault and were glad to change into dry comfy clothing and sit down with a warm drink on the sofa together.

William automatically put his arm

around her and drew her down so she nestled against his chest. The fire flickered and there was a sense of peace about the place, which he had not felt since arriving in the parish.

Revd Tully had always made it quite clear he liked the house to be kept his way — everything in the place he had put it and nothing to be unduly disturbed. The same philosophy had applied to his order of services and traditional content. He had no time for anything modern; he only wanted the old, tried and tested form of Christianity.

William felt that there had been a defensiveness about him. When William suggested involving children and teenagers in more family orientated services and activities he had been reluctant, even though he knew he should.

Likewise, the thought of holding a healing service and moving the focus towards the Holy Spirit, had brought about a reaction so strong that William felt as though he had suggested introducing a seance to the proceedings.

In short, William had decided that the Revd Tully was threatened by change and was unwilling or unable to keep up.

As William sipped his drink and stroked Susan's hair he pondered the task of introducing those changes gently now the way had been made clear for him.

It would not be easy, as there were many like Tully, and Arthur, who based their Christianity on the lifelong familiarity of set protocol and services. Somehow he had to embrace them and the new order of the day, if the church was to strive and survive. Then he chuckled to himself — new order. The Holy Spirit is far from new.

'What are you thinking about, Will?' Sue grinned mischievously at him, 'Remembering Paris?'

'Not exactly. Are you warm enough?' William looked down at her face as she let her head slide on to his chest.

'No.' She reached up with open arms

and wrapped them around his neck bringing his lips towards hers.

He felt a warmth stir within him as he responded, finding her lips with his and letting his senses fill as they kissed, the passion ringing within both as they lay entwined on the sofa.

Burr, Burr . . .

'The phone!' He sat up.

'Leave it.'

'I can't. The answer phone is on . . . your message.' William dashed over and lifted up the receiver. He heard Sue sigh as he did.

'Hello, William speaking.'

'I'm glad it is, although from the message I've just heard it could have been anyone, certainly not a Vicar!'

'Hello, Arthur. It is my day off and . . . ' William paused as he heard Sue stomp upstairs followed by her door being shut firmly behind her.

'Yes, I'm well aware of that. I wanted to know how your sick sheep was?'

William was lost between two words. 'I'm sorry?'

'Emily, is she in hospital?'

William sat on the stairs and told him how Emily was. As he replaced the receiver and changed his answering message on the machine, he glanced up at the door of the guest bedroom and thought of his past, delicious as it was.

Then he looked around at the gloom of the vicarage and thought of his present and the work he had ahead of him to change what was there.

From despondency he felt a strange sensation of challenge. Somehow I'll make it happen. God willing! Then I can get on with what I really want to do. Go where I can make a difference to the truly deprived.

5

Carole held on firmly as Jason pedalled along the promenade enjoying the feelings of girlish excitement that were sweeping through her. He was strong and fit, just like her hero had been, but she doubted that he was nimble enough to climb up rigging or swoop on to the poop deck as he used to in the series.

Jason was too solid now for that. Middle age had made his once slim figure, stockier. It was all she could do not to call him First Lieutenant Malachi Smart.

'Go up there,' Carole shouted above the noise of the passing traffic and pointed to a narrow street that cut through the row of Victorian seafront hotels. They wobbled slightly as he pedalled the bike hard into the wind to change direction until they reached the shelter of Lord Street.

For a moment she thought she heard him laugh, but decided it was more of a gasp. He freewheeled over to the kerb and dismounted. Jason was slightly short of breath after his exertion.

Carole noticed his cheeks were flushed red, which made him even more attractive. She was lost in admiration. It took all her willpower not to put her hand out to touch his face to make sure he really was there. Carole felt so happy, that unfamiliar emotions welled up inside her threatening to burst out.

She bit her bottom lip and tried to control herself when suddenly she was overcome with new feelings — she sensed fear and disappointment rising within her. Was that it? Was he going to leave as quickly as he had entered her life?

'Thank you for your help.' He did not look at her but continued to fold up her cagoule and hand it back.

'Where will you go?' Carole tried not to betray the desperate need she felt for him to stay with her. Just for a while longer — *or the rest of my life!*

'Collect my bag I suppose, from the hotel. Take a taxi to an airport and then Paris, Zurich or Rome. Wherever I go they always find me.'

'Only if you do what they'd expect you to do,' Carole said trying not to betray the desperation she was feeling within her.

Jason put his hands deep into the pockets of his leather jacket and tilted his head on one side, looking at her as if he had just seen her for the first time. 'What would you suggest then?'

'You really have a problem with trusting people.' Carole smiled warmly at him. 'Come with me, to a place where no self-respecting international superstar would be seen.'

She felt in control again. Jason was tempted; she could see it in his face. Not by her. Carole knew she was too short, possibly too heavy at a size twelve, well, sometimes a fourteen, depending on the cut, and too old by about fifteen years for his current preferences. But he was tempted by the offer none the less.

'You're mocking me, aren't you?' His deep, relaxed voice had not changed over the years. 'Where had you in mind?' he asked, reluctantly putting on the cheap waterproof over his beautifully made jacket.

'A cabin along the coast road from here. No frills and no mod-cons. Ideal for 'finding oneself' when lost. It's called the Captain's Retreat. I've seen it advertised on our notice board.'

'Whose notice board is that?' There it was again — suspicion.

Carole ignored the patronising tone in his voice.

'The one in our church. The ad said that the cabin offers a place of seclusion, but it costs a hundred pounds in February — off season.' I'd already be there if I'd had the money, Carole thought, but was glad as she looked up at Jason that she had not been able to afford it.

'You cannot be serious.' Jason hesitated for a moment, then, as the rain started again, he zipped up the cagoule once more. 'What the hell. OK. But at that price, only for a couple of nights.'

'It's a hundred pounds for a week's rent off season, not a night!' Carole said grinning broadly as Jason had obviously got the wrong idea.

'Does it have hot and cold running water?' he asked sarcastically as he put his hand back on the handlebars of the bike.

'I presume so, but I've never stayed there, so it will be an adventure for both of us.'

'Let's go somewhere out of the wet where we can talk.' Jason held the handlebars as if to take control.

Yes! 'OK,' Carol said calmly. 'but we have to return William's bike first.'

'Who's William?' Jason asked. 'Is he coming too? We could sell tickets if you wish. Then the press would never suspect a thing.' He grinned and once more the rain increased its intensity. As it poured down once more Carole quickly stood on the pedals. 'Let me. I know where I'm going.'

'Glad somebody does.' Jason sat on the seat, not quite sure that to do with his feet.

'Hang on, it's quite near.'

'What is?'

Carole didn't answer. She pushed off with Jason holding on to her waist for dear life. The rain poured but she didn't really care. Reality had disappeared. She felt as if nothing could dampen her spirits, not even the torrential rain.

Five minutes later she pedalled up the narrow alley that took them back to St Bede's church. They dismounted and Carole half pushed him into the shelter of a small hall doorway that stood behind the old eighteenth century church. She quickly fumbled for a key and opened the door.

Inside she leant the dripping bike against a wall and for the first time felt totally at ease. The hall was old and run down. It had seen better days as its faded and scuffed walls easily told. With her bedraggled hair and sodden clothes she felt an empathy with it.

'It's not much but it offers shelter and hospitality for young and old alike. We hope to build a new one eventually,' Carole offered as an apologetic explanation for their humble surroundings.

'We, being you and William, I presume,' Jason said as he glanced around, obviously unimpressed.

'You shouldn't make presumptions then. I meant 'we' as in the members of the church. William is the Curate. It's his day off. So I borrowed his bike as it's such a pain parking near the pier.'

She felt colour flush her cheeks as he coupled her name with William's. He raised a quizzical eyebrow at her. She really didn't want to offend him, but he had a very opinionated way of putting things that she found herself rising to.

Carole glanced up at the hall clock. 'Look, if you really don't want to be seen we had better get moving. My car is over there; I'll go and pick up some things and then we can phone about the cabin.' Carole took the card advertising the Captain's Retreat from the notice board and showed it to him.

He ran his hand through his hair again. Carole thought it must be a nervous habit he had.

'Look, I appreciate your offer, but if you could just take me back to the hotel I'll make my plans from there.' He handed her the card back.

Carole could feel a lump in her throat. However, she forced a smile and put the card in her pocket. If it really was not needed then she would return it to the board later. Whilst he was with her there was still a chance that he might decide to come. She nodded at him and said, 'Just as you like.'

Carole locked the door and told herself she had already been very fortunate. Some people dream of meeting their hero and never come within a mile of them. She had held him fleetingly, and he her. They had shared an intimate moment together. Two people lost in their own thoughts and time. She should be grateful. The rain still poured so they ran over to the car park passing the back of the church.

She felt a huge pang of guilt as she glanced up at the cross silhouetted against the grey sky. Oh God, be with me, but let me live a little for once.

They ran over to where a silver grey BMW was parked. Jason ran to the passenger door and placed his hand on the handle ready to open it.

She continued running and tried to look as if she hadn't noticed the totally bemused expression cross his face as she continued around it to her old two-tone Mini parked at the other side.

Russet and rust was how she normally described it. She rushed to the passenger side and opened the door for him, then climbing in the driver's seat. She sat behind the large wheel and pulled the choke out.

'I don't know if you're a religious man, Mr Forbes, but I usually pray at, this point as the rain sometimes causes a slight problem with the distributor cap.' Carole did not look at Jason who was trying to find room for his legs in the front. 'There's a bar under the seat; if you squeeze it up you can slide the seat right back.'

'Is this thing a real car or a Matchbox model?' Jason asked sarcastically as he released the seat and shot back all of six inches.

The car started first time and Carole grinned broadly with pride and relief. She glanced at the small gap between the top of Jason's head and the roof. 'You've got a long back,' she commented.

'No, not really. You have a short car!' Jason was smiling as he spoke. Whatever he was used to, the change seemed to be doing him good as he looked altogether more relaxed as he fumbled with the seat belt.

'I suppose you drive a bigger one.' Carole thought of all the fancy cars she knew about — Lotus, Porsche, Ferrari that was about the extent of her, knowledge or interest in such things.

'I would say that was a good and an educated guess as it would be difficult

to find a smaller one. I have a Lexus.'
Jason finally clicked the seat belt into
place as he spoke.

'Is that Korean — one of the Daewoo
range?' Carole asked as she made her
way along the promenade towards The
Grand Hotel.

Jason laughed, openly wiping a tear
from his eyes. 'You really have no idea
have you?' Then as they turned into the
hotel's car park his smile dropped.
'How did you know where I was staying
if you've not been following me?'

'Well, this is the only five star hotel
we have and somehow I didn't think
you would book into The Sea View
Guest House.' Carole stopped the
engine; she always felt protective of her
little car and didn't like it being
ridiculed. She had owned it for fifteen
years and it was all she could afford.

She placed her hand on the handle of
the door ready to open it when he
placed his hand on her left arm. A
feeling of joy swept through her.

'Look.' He pointed to a car that was

pulling up outside the main door. Two men climbed out, both carrying photographic equipment. 'You'll have to go in and collect my bag. Phone down to the desk from the room and ask them to prepare my bill and have it sent up to the room straight away. I'll have to wait here.' His face was very serious and he looked ill at ease again.

Carole stared at Jason's worried face and marvelled how quickly it could change moods, like the sea. He really did not want to be found, of that she was sure. Brilliant! 'Excuse me.'

Carole touched his leg gently as she fumbled in her glove compartment for her small hairbrush. She tried to ignore the sweep of sensations that ran through her as the thought of who she was touching delighted her. Next she produced her lipstick and quickly put that on. She suddenly became very self-conscious as she realised that Jason was staring at her.

'Every little helps!' she smiled nervously.

'Indeed, but it's not you they're looking out for.' He held out a piece of plastic that looked like a plain credit card.

'What's that for?' Carole asked.

'That is my room key, number 507.'

'Really.' Carole turned it over in her hand fascinated by it. 'Don't they use proper keys anymore then?' she asked inquisitively, then cringed as she realised she was showing yet more ignorance of the broader world.

Carole placed the key safely in her pocket then, with as much confidence as she could muster looked up at Jason's obviously humoured face. 'I'll be as quick as I can.' She left him skulking awkwardly in her little car, desperate not to be seen.

Carole was glad she had her black slacks on and not her old jeans, even if they were wet. She made straight for the lifts, by crossing the beautifully tiled foyer as quickly as possible. It was whilst she was waiting for the lift to arrive that she noticed the sign. *South*

East Photographic Society — Conference in Progress.

She looked at the key in her hand and was about to turn back to the car to tell Jason that the photographers were not waiting for him, when the lift arrived. A smile crossed her face as she pressed the button for the fifth floor. Well I would not be lying if I just didn't say anything about it.

She soon found the door and could barely stop her hand from shaking as she slid the piece of plastic into the slot. The door released itself from the catch and Carole slowly pushed it open. Wow! The room was large and golden in décor.

A sumptuous carpet softened her tread as she entered. He obviously had not intended to stay long because a black leather bag was left unpacked on the side-table near the bed. Carole phoned down for his bill as she had been instructed and stressed that Mr Forbes was in a hurry to leave.

The view from the window overlooked the pier, where what seemed like an age ago their paths had crossed. She checked all the drawers and wardrobes to make sure nothing was left behind. Carole looked at the bag and wondered what was inside. Should she take a peek? A knock at the door made her jump with guilt.

'Mr Forbes' account.' The man in the smart navy and green uniform held a small silver tray out towards her.

'Thank you,' she said and smiled taking the tray and wondering if in fact she should have just picked up the bill from on top of it.

When Carole returned to the foyer carrying the heavy bag there was a group of six photographers just leaving the hotel. She followed them out and crossed over to the car. Opening the passenger door she handed him his bag. To her surprise he took it from her eagerly and held it in front of him, obscuring part of his view.

He's hiding from them. 'Where to?' Carole asked.

'Phone that retreat place; if it's

vacant I'll stay there a few days until they lose the scent, then I'll leave.'

Yes! Carole started up the Mini and drove back out on to the promenade. 'I'll have to pick up a few things and make a call. Then we'll get you safely away.' Carole looked round at him. Still gorgeous after all this time. 'Don't worry, you're safe with me,' she said comfortingly.

'Oh good,' he replied sounding totally unconvinced, but Carole thought she saw a smile cross his face. The rain stopped and the sun shone brighter than Carole thought it had for years.

6

For a moment William pondered whether he should go and talk to Sue, or let her cool off and look at tomorrow's sermon. At least he was free to preach God's message in his own way now.

William preferred using props and congregation interaction rather than straight preaching. His past experience in marketing seemed to be paying off. He did have a way of communicating with people. William had great respect for the older core of the congregation; in his way of thinking no-one should 'have' to change their ways with the times. It was his job to make them want to change, if in fact it was the right thing to do. He was only too aware that change for its own sake was a folly.

A loud banging on the door stopped his thoughts.

'George! I didn't expect to see you today.'

'No, well you wouldn't on your day off.' George grinned, but held up his tool bag. 'I've come to fix your bell, Bill. What better day to catch you in than today. Besides, it won't take me two ticks. You carry on doing what you were doing and I'll be out of your hair in no time.'

'Right, thanks.' William turned around to continue what he was doing. Decision time! 'I'd offer you a drink but we're going out soon.'

'Oh yes, I forgot you had a friend staying. Sorry, well it's only the wiring so it'll only be a minute's job.'

William bounded up the stairs two at a time. He rapped tunefully on Sue's door. She ignored it so he gave one firmer knock. It opened.

'Sue, put one of your new outfits on. We're going out.' William was leaning with a raised arm on the doorframe. Sue looked up at him, standing only an inch from his broad chest. He stroked her cheek gently with the finger of his other hand.

'I love it when you're so masterful.'

'Stop talking and get changed. We're going out where nobody can find me.'

'Where would that be?' Sue asked as she wrapped her arms around him and he responded by holding her to him.

Sweet temptation, I never wanted to be a monk. 'You choose, but no London theatres OK?' William kissed her forehead gently.

'Take me to the cinema and then a meal.' Sue stepped back and William laughed.

'The pictures — crumbs it's ages since I saw a film. What do you want to see?' He folded his arms as she walked back into her bedroom and opened the old wardrobe door.

'Every time I open this thing I expect moths or bats to fly out. It's ancient!' Sue said as she stepped back to study the contents.

'It came with the property. What do you want to see?'

'Something funny like *Bridget Jones*.' Sue grinned.

'Who is she?'

'A fictitious lady who finds romance.'

'Is it a comedy or a tragedy?' William asked.

'Oh, a comedy. The girl who gets her man. Now if you'll excuse me, Vicar, I must dress.'

'Call a truce, Sue and you shall see your film, and have a Chinese afterwards.' William turned to go.

'That will make a change. I hope it's Jackie Chan!' Sue giggled.

'No, a takeaway.' He left her, listening to her infectious girlie laughter. She was fickle, beautifully shallow in her desires in life and completely at odds with his beliefs. But right now she was precisely what he needed — or wanted.

Bing-bong. William returned to George, who was standing proudly pressing a fully functional doorbell.

'Thanks, George.'

'No charge, no problem.' George smiled and left as swiftly as he had appeared.

'Sue, hurry up. We're escaping before anything else happens.'

Just then the phone rang. Sue appeared at the top of the stairs wearing a long navy jersey skirt and loose cotton knit jumper, a small leather bag slung casually over her shoulder and her blonde locks bouncing carefree. 'Answer that and I'm packing my bag this minute!'

Sue's ultimatum was totally unnecessary. 'The answer phone is on, so let's go.' He cupped her elbow in his hand and firmly locked the vicarage door behind him.

Sue insisted she bought the tickets whilst he loitered in some dark corner of the large ten-screen cinema foyer. She had no intention of any of his flock spotting him.

William watched her walk over to him with an added bounce to her step. She had an almost childlike quality to her — or should that be childish?

'Come on, Will. Let's find a cosy seat at the back.'

'Lead on.' William was more than glad to let someone else make the decisions for once, even at such a simple level.

William watched the film. The morals were light and the story fun. If only he could get the aimless youths he was trying to help to take control positively of their lives. With God's help he could.

We need to put our message over in a humorous way, but without detracting from the seriousness of it. The West is filled with cynics! How to break through the cynicism to let people, especially the young, openly show their faith without ridicule.

'There, I told you it was a brilliant film and moralistic too!' Sue said triumphantly before turning to him and planting a passionate kiss firmly on his lips. He responded, embracing her in kind. Then the lights came on and Sue pulled away.

'I'm starving. Which restaurant are we going to?' she asked, eyes wide with enthusiasm.

'Restaurant?' William looked at her and grinned.

'The Chinese. Remember? You promised,' Sue reminded him.

'Takeaway.' William pulled a sheepish face.

'Oh, no you don't,' Sue said and stood up, pulling him up by his hand. 'You are coming to a proper restaurant, regardless of who pays. I'm not getting cosy sat around your fire, chopsticks at the ready, for some old biddy to call you away again. Tonight you are mine. Where's the nearest Chinese restaurant?'

'The Golden Dragon,' William answered, as he put his arm around her shoulder and walked her back to the car.

'You're too good for this, you know?' Sue said solemnly as they reached his old Renault.

'Too good for what, Sue?' William asked as he opened the door for her to get in.

'Too handsome for a curate or whatever.' Sue put her hand on his knee as he sat in the driver's seat.

'Are all curates ugly then?' William grinned at her.

'How would I know? You're the first one I've met. But don't they hate having fun and read all those serious sermons. You're too normal.' Sue leant her head on his shoulder.

'Normal?' William repeated.

'You know what I mean,' Sue persisted.

'I'm not sure I do.' William turned the key on and the engine provided a comforting distraction to him.

'You like normal things. You used to like to have fun and party and you loved making lots of money and being a success.'

'I used to crave those things, but I've changed — grown. Let's go back to our truce Sue and I'm starving. Do you still want to eat?' William looked at her and she replaced her pout with her sweetest smile.

'Yes.'

7

Conversation was difficult as Carole drove along the broad avenue lined with cherry trees with large detached and semi-detached houses at either side. Each four or five bedroom home was tastefully different in design and space from their neighbours.

To Carole they were very impressive, a far cry from the council house she had grown up in but Jason seemed to stare blankly out of the window lost in his own world of thought as they left the seafront and pier behind them.

Eventually the roads became narrower and the houses smaller until she turned into the drive of a three-bedroomed semi. It had a spacious garden, back and front, and was built in the pre-war period when houses had individual rooms with doors, entrance halls that guaranteed privacy and a small bedroom that you could get a decent three-foot bed in, unlike the modern boxes of today.

'You live here?' Jason asked, as if he was surprised at the idea.

'Yes,' Carole answered proudly. 'Come inside and I'll make you a cup of tea whilst I phone the Retreat.'

'Don't you have a job, or something you should be doing?' He looked at her raising one eyebrow. Without moving from the car, he watched her reaction carefully as if doubting her motives once more.

'You really do have a trust problem. Come on in and I'll explain.' Carole climbed out of the car and unlocked the door of the house. Jason followed her. When she turned to speak to him she could see he was taking in all the details of the décor as he walked along the hall.

He stopped and ran his hand along the highly-polished mahogany stair rail. Its darkness was in stark contrast to the cream embossed wallpaper that shimmered with a gold and silvery fleck, whilst under foot the parquet flooring seemed to balance the two.

'The kitchen is through the door straight ahead of you. If you put the kettle on I'll make the call. Should I book it in my name?' Carole asked him feeling rather unsure that she really understood what she was doing. Although, looking at him standing there, tall and 'real' in front of her — Yes, this is real. He is here, she did not have to question why she was throwing all rational, sane thoughts to the wind.

She welcomed back the young girl she had once been and all the child's frivolous dreams. They were standing in front of her, looking straight back from the dark brown eyes of Jason. Only he did not know how she felt and he must not. If he did, the girl who dreamed would be shattered leaving only an embarrassed shell of a woman.

Jason smiled. 'It might be a good idea, if I'm to remain hidden in this place.'

'Good idea,' Carole repeated and

blushed slightly. 'It's a hundred pounds up front . . . I think it will have to be cash at such short notice. Is that a problem, Mr Forbes?'

'Not to me. No. Why should it be to you when you live in a house like this?' Again the suspicion.

'The house belongs to my sister and her husband. I have a room next to Tom's and I help them out for my board and a small allowance. Any extra I earn working part-time jobs when I can fit them in.'

'I thought you were an illustrator?' Jason asked as he folded his arms and leant against the hall paper. Judy would have a fit! Carole couldn't help thinking of the reaction Judy would have if she could see him leaning a damp coat against her golden-flecked flock. Not even Jason Forbes would get away with that without a ticking off. She quickly took him by the arm and directed him into the kitchen.

'I illustrate things, like the church magazine and such, but it doesn't pay.

It's just a hobby.' Carole filled the kettle and sat him at the oak table in her favourite chair next to the Aga. It was always warm there. Then she quickly ran back and checked the wall wasn't stained. It felt slightly damp but she decided it would dry out OK.

As she phoned the number for the Retreat her hand was trembling with the excitement. Please let it be free! It rang three times then a kindly sounding lady answered the phone. She could not believe her luck. The Retreat had been empty and the lady was so pleased to receive a booking.

It was free and they would accept cash on arrival. Quickly she jotted down details of where she had to go to get the key for it and pay them the money. The directions to the cabin sounded simple, if not a little vague, but Carole didn't care.

If she lost her way, she would be lost with Jason Forbes. Yes! Excitedly she rushed back into the kitchen. He looked as though he had been about to nod off when she flung the door open.

'It's free!' she said, as she went over to the kettle to make the tea. She couldn't hide her enthusiasm and delight.

'Oh good!' he said sombrely, almost as if in a deliberately opposing tone. 'Does that mean we don't have to pay or is it just vacant?'

Carole could not see the patronising look on his face as she bustled about getting Judy's best cups and teapot out. She laughed at his joke, oblivious to him watching her.

'No, you've got to pay, I'm afraid. Cash on arrival. I have the instructions of where to go and how to get there and I'll take a map and torch with us.'

'Torch?'

'Well yes, by the time I've packed a few things, phoned Mrs Henderson and Judy and driven to collect the key, it will be quite late when we arrive.' Carole put his tea in front of him, then placed some biscuits on a plate.

Jason then asked, 'Who's Mrs Henderson?'

'She is the lady who is looking after Tom today. I'll see if she'll take him until the weekend and then Judy can organise him after that.'

'Judy being your sister, and Tom her son?' Jason tucked into some biscuits.

'Yes. I won't be long.' Carole flew upstairs, grabbed her holdall and shoved some jumpers, jeans, T-shirts, undies and toiletries into her bag. Once convinced she had everything she needed to survive a spell in a coastal cabin in February, she phoned Mrs Henderson and arranged for her to look after Tom for a couple of days. Satisfied she had done all she could to help Judy cope with her sudden disappearance, Carole then phoned William.

A feeling of guilt seemed to fill her. Am I being a fool? Is this right? Do I even care? Her heightened feelings answered all her questions or at least overruled her more sane answers that advised of caution, discretion and propriety.

The answerphone was on. William's

disembodied voice asked her to leave a message. Carole was relieved. If William had questioned where she was going and why, she would have told him for sure. Then he would have stopped her and helped Jason himself.

He wouldn't mean to stop Carole from having fun but William helped people whenever and wherever he could. That was William; it was what he did. It was his total lack of selfishness that made him such a special and admirable person to Carole. But everybody loved him, and everybody had their share of him.

Carole increasingly needed someone of her own to love and to love her back. At least this way she would be gone before he had even heard the message.

Life is for living and it's time I did. 'William, it's Carole. I'm taking a little vacation and won't be around for a week — perhaps two. I'm fine — just needed a change. Will phone when I get back. Bye.'

Oh help. Now — time to tell Judy.

Reluctantly Carole picked up the receiver and phoned Judy's number. She knew Judy didn't like her phoning her in the office unless it was very important, like an emergency, but to Carole this was.

Carole took a deep breath as she heard the phone was answered. 'Hi Judy I . . .'

'What's wrong? Is it Tom?' Judy's voice was filled with panic straight away.

'No, he's OK.' Carole sounded as calm as she could under the circumstances.

'Then why are you phoning me at work? I'm preparing a report and . . .'

'Judy, I've arranged for Mrs Henderson to look after Tom for you for the next three days.' Mrs Henderson was a close friend of the family. She had known her mother and was like a surrogate gran for Tom. Carole had grown up calling her Mrs Henderson; it seemed disrespectful to call her Mary.

'Whatever for? Mary only has him

today because today's your day off. Are you ill?' Judy sounded cross rather than concerned.

Carole felt like saying 'yes' just to hear the response. She was never ill and had always been there for Judy and Tom. Perhaps I've been there too much for them. A holiday, Carole thought, was justified.

'No, I'm not ill. I've decided to take a few days off. I'm having a holiday.'

'Just like that — you can't!' Carole was shocked and hurt, but most of all annoyed. She had brought Judy up during their mother's illness and helped her throughout her schooling, since her death.

She helped her go to college and then supported her with Tom, making it easy for her to carry on with her career. Carole had never suddenly taken time off at short notice before, but with Jason sitting in her kitchen, she was not going to let this dream or reality pass her by, not even for Judy.

'Yes, I can — and Judy — I am. I'll

be in touch and let you know when I'm coming back. I need a holiday.' Carole put down the receiver firmly and tried to let the angry colour fade from her cheeks before returning to the kitchen, when Jason's voice surprised her.

'She wasn't very pleased then?' He grinned broadly at her. Carole laughed back as there was no use denying that the call had been difficult.

'We'd better get out of here before she arrives home in a blinding temper.' Carole picked up her car keys from the hall table.

'Do you think I'd be frightened of her?' Jason asked.

'No. Mr Forbes, I don't. However, she would see you and discretion is not part of her character when she has just had her domestic bliss spoiled!' Carole then picked up her holdall and walked to the door.

'You'd better call me Jason, if we are to cohabit.'

Carole did not look up at him but sensed the mockery in his voice. When he was away from the threat of the Press he was starting to relax and enjoy their adventure.

Once safely back outside, Carole decided that she should too. She placed her bag in the small boot and held her hand out for Jason's. He stared at the small cavity and looked soulfully at her.

'Perhaps if we put yours in first, I might be able to shove mine in at the end. It's surprising what will fit in with a bit of manoeuvring and care.' Carole sounded confident but could not hide her grin, as the boot was very small.

'Just a minute.' Jason placed his bag on the open boot door and Carole leaped forward, picking it up and moving it on to the more secure floor of the boot itself.

'It's an old car.' She offered her explanation feeling both embarrassed and defensive of her little 'Rusty'. She was trying really hard not to talk to it like she normally did when it was temperamental. The last thing she wanted was for Jason to think he had landed himself in the hands of a raving mad woman, in any sense of the word.

'Should I rent a proper car or does this Matchbox version carry any guarantees.' Jason muttered sarcastically as he unzipped his bag.

'It gets me where I want to go. Besides it's cheap, if you haven't got the extra money to throw around.'

Jason pulled out of his bag a bound leather case, which at first she thought was a lavish Filofax, but it was larger and completely sealed. Then he produced a mobile phone and a wallet. Carole tried not to stare and made sure that when he re-zipped his bag and stood up again she was looking across the road.

'It's safe for you to look now,' he said with a dry humour to his vice, but Carole noticed that his eyes appeared to have sparkle to them that had previously been lacking. 'Now you can fit both bags into your cavernous boot.' He walked around to the passenger side with his belongings and climbed in.

Carole quickly locked the boot and sat in the driver's seat, switching the engine on straight away.

'Now before we go anywhere let me give you this.' He started to open the wallet he had removed from his bag.

'Sorry, we've got to get out of here. Judy will be in such a rage she's certain to be making her way home to try to talk some sense into me.' Before he had time to clip his belt on she reversed out and started driving back down to the coast road.

'What's the rush? I could handle your big sis,' Jason told Carole as she put her foot down until they had turned a few corners and had several roads between them and her home.

'She's not my big sister. I'm hers.' Carole glanced at him, feeling rather awkward as the declaration of sibling pecking order made her feel as though she was a wimp. 'Belt up!' Carole ordered as she slowed down.

'I beg your pardon?' Jason sounded so pompous that Carole openly laughed.

'Your belt — fasten it, please.'

'Oh, well I would have if you hadn't put Matchbox into jet speed. Does it do warp factor or just start-stop?'

'It goes. Well, most of the time. Rain getting into his engine is the worst flaw he has. If you must call him a name you may as well call him 'Rusty'.' Carole blushed slightly as he laughed and fumbled with the manual adjustment on the seat belt.

'OK. Now you've made your escape. Let's get a few things sorted out.' Jason put the black leather case carefully down on the rubber foot mat by his feet.

'What's that?' Carole asked glancing curiously at the case.

'Things like food, rent, confidentiality . . . '

'No, I mean what's in that case?' Carole persisted not really listening to what he was saying.

'A lap-top,' Jason told her as if a child should have known.

'Really, I've always thought they must

be a brilliant thing to have. I mean when you think of the size of a proper computer.'

'It is a 'proper' computer. Can we get back to what I was talking about? We will need food unless this 'cabin' is fully fitted with everything to accommodate our creature comforts. Which somehow I doubt.'

Carole shrugged her shoulders. She also doubted there would be much there. That's why she picked up a torch, matches and a few candles. Just in case. 'I thought we could stop at the big supermarket on the edge of town and get some supplies. Trouble is I don't know how big the fridge is.'

'We can always leave food outside; it's certainly cold enough.' Jason remarked in a droll voice.

'Well we could but it would have to be well wrapped or the animals will ravish it.'

'I was joking.' Jason opened his wallet and pulled out four fifty-pound notes. 'There are two for the rent and two for our food. You do all the washing up, OK?'

'Right — agreed,' Carole answered enthusiastically. 'Write down what you like to eat and I'll get the shopping.'

By the time they reached the supermarket Jason had completed a full list of his food and drink options. When Carole read it she did not like to ask him what some of the items were, like *abalone*. She thought she would ask in the supermarket instead. Even the wine had names other than red, white, claret.

Carole parked Rusty away from the other cars. 'I'll be as quick as I can.'

'Leave me the keys, map and directions,' Jason said and held out his hand for the car keys.

Carole hesitated. She really did not know this man at all. Yet here she was trusting him with her biggest and most treasured possession. Her beloved Rusty.

'You really have a trust problem, don't you?' He grinned at her as he returned her own phrase back on her. There he was again, her hero. More wrinkled and thick set than once those lovely lean features had once been but the eyes still had it.

Oh William, I hope I know what I'm doing. Shaken by her own sudden thoughts of William and wondered why she should be thinking of him at a time like this, she tossed her beloved keys into his hand.

Jason turned them over and read the key fob out loud. *If you want anything said, ask a man. If you want anything done, ask a woman.* He looked up at her. 'Woman, you had better do the shopping or it will be midnight before we reach the Retreat.'

It took Carole forty long minutes to hunt down all the things on the list and also a few of her own favourites. As usual she had picked the trolley with crab-like tendencies and the checkout with the problem customer. I hate food shopping! When flustered and fraught she finally made it back to the car park her heart sank.

Had it all been a fantasy of an early

mid-life crisis. Had she imagined Jason? If so how did she get to where she was now, standing in a car park with a load of groceries and a shopping list written in a very grand style. But he'd gone and taken Rusty with him.

She would rather have never seen him than lose her car. It was the only thing she possessed of worth. Then she heard him. His little beep. Carole looked to her right. He had moved Rusty near to where the cash point machines were. She beamed at him as she struggled with the trolley.

Opening the driver's door she loaded the bags of shopping behind their seats and on the back seat of Rusty. 'No room for this in the boot. I knew you wouldn't desert me.'

'No, you didn't,' Jason said, his eyes challenging her to deny it.

'OK, I thought you'd conned me and taken my car.'

'You're a terrible liar . . . ' he said.

'I am not! I don't lie. Well, not often and . . . '

'Not at all well. That is what I meant. You are terrible at lying, not that you're a terrible or frequent liar. You certainly would not be a convincing member of the paparrazi.'

'I'll take that as a compliment,' Carole said as she put the last bag in.

'Believe me, it was meant as one.' Jason had the map in front of him. 'You drive and I'll read the map. That way, we may actually find this place. OK?'

'Yes, that's fine with me.' Carole drove out on to the coast road thinking that it was more than fine with her.

8

The coast road was fairly dull as the sea wall protected the low-lying ground from high tides, obscuring the view. So Carole kept driving along the straight and unswerving road until the sky which had been cloudy all day turned into a gloomier and darker evening.

Much of the land to the right was rough, grassy land that occasionally turned marshy. At least the rain had held off so Rusty had been saved a struggle against driving water. Birds loved the open rough land but few people wanted to live there.

After driving for an hour, leaving most town dwelling inhabitants behind them, they both seemed pleased to see the sea as the road crept up a gentle hill to higher ground. Controlled grassed slopes and farmland now replaced the low marshland.

Carole had driven in silence most of the way. It appeared to be a time of realisation and adjustment for both of them. Jason closed his eyes and, in the absence of a headrest, was leaning his head against the window. He appeared to have nodded off and Carole was glad the road was so straight, allowing her the luxury of glancing at him, amazed that he was there, in her car.

As the road steepened and turned away from the coast, it passed through a forested area where houses were interspersed in their own secluded part of the woodland. 'Jason, I think we must be near.' Carole spoke gently so as not to wake him suddenly.

'Turn left at the fork up ahead.' Carole realised that he had been watching her progress through heavy lids. He straightened the map on his knee and reread the instructions the friendly lady had given Carole on the phone. Carole turned left and the road dipped down a single unlit road immediately on the right. She put

Rusty's lights on full and groaned at the state of the track that lay ahead. She stopped the car.

'I'm sorry, Mr Forbes — Jason.' Embarrassed at her lack of confidence and Rusty's inability to cope in certain situations, she looked at Jason.

'Sorry for what? Is this the end of the road or are you planning to rob me here in the depth of the woods — or worse?' He smiled until he saw her pull the torch out from under her seat. Next she pulled out a Wellington boot also from under her seat.

'Excuse me.' She put her hand down and reached under his seat for her other boot.

'You really should've been a Girl Guide. I think you missed your vocation, you'd have gone far.' Jason spoke as he swiftly grabbed his laptop, saving it from any contact with Carole's boot as she pulled it free.

Carole slipped off her Hush Puppies and manoeuvred her wellies on to her feet. Then she opened the car door only to shut it quickly. 'I'm sorry.'

'Yes, you've already said that, but you have not said why you are so sorry.' His face told her that although he found her behaviour humorous or perhaps just peculiar, he was also concerned. There was a problem.

'It's Rusty — he's not a four-wheeled vehicle.'

'He was when we got into it. Did something drop off or do you mean he's not a 4×4 wheeled vehicle?' His voice was light-hearted but that did not help Carole's embarrassment or her dilemma.

'Whatever.' Carole shrugged her shoulders dismissively. 'Rusty cannot go further down here or he'll get stuck in the mud or lose his exhaust or something. Which means we have to walk to the door and collect the key to the Retreat.'

'Wrong!' Jason sounded confident and firm.

'Right. I know him. I know his limits.' Carole was adamant.

'Yes and I know mine. I'm not walking through mud in shoes that cost me . . . ' he paused and looked at her, 'well never mind. I'm staying. You and your Wellingtons can collect the key. I'll babysit Rusty for you.'

'That is not very gallant of you, is it?' Carole thought of her hero struggling through swamps to rescue the captive crew, risking life and limb to man, beast and malaria, then stared at the comfortable, stubborn, gorgeous none-the-less, infuriating man in her car.

'I'm not used to walking through dark woods in the middle of the night.' Carole admitted this but was surprised when all he did was grin at her.

'No, would it surprise you to know that neither am I and it is the middle of the evening, not the night.' Jason leaned across and opened her door for her. 'The sooner you go, the sooner you will return and we can drive to this luxury haven for the night.'

Carole put one foot out of the car, then suddenly inspiration hit. She leaned into the back and pulled out two carrier bags from the supermarket shopping.

She always took a couple of extras as she found them such useful things. 'You could put these over your shoes and tie them around your trousers so they wouldn't get messed up.' She smiled at him, impressed by her own ingenuity.

Jason picked up the torch and plonked it firmly on her knee. 'I do not wear carrier bags. Bye.'

Carole got out without saying a word. Then before shutting the door she bent down and said, 'You could always pretend you were a hero helping a maiden in distress, you know — act the part.'

'I only act when I'm paid to. Bye.' He slumped down resting his head against the car door and closing his eyes.

With that she shut Rusty's door and set off down the track. That man's as stubborn as Thomas is! When the path ahead bent to the left she hoped to see the bungalow, but there was no sign of

119

it so she stopped. William would never have let me go on alone.

Feeling annoyed and desperate, in a fit of madness and determination, she let out a scream and then waited. Five minutes later Jason appeared sliding around the bend, carrier bags firmly tied over his shoes and knotted over his trouser bottoms. 'What happened?'

'Pardon?' Carole asked innocently as she pointed the torch to guide his way to her.

'You screamed!' He was standing by her; concern was turning into the realisation that he had been conned.

'I slipped, but it's nice to know you care. Come on, I think we've about half a mile to walk. Did you lock Rusty up?'

Jason narrowed his eyes as if he would consider murder or turning back. 'Who's going to steal that tin toy out here? The food would be of more value.'

Then he looked up at the sky and the trees. 'We'd better get that blasted key.' Without hesitation he took the torch from her and held her hand as he led the way down to the path to the old bungalow. The muddy track that had seemed to pull at her wellies with every step she took suddenly seemed to offer her no resistance at all as she walked along with Jason — hand in hand.

After ten minutes steady progress they saw a gate and then a small bungalow almost overgrown by creeping ivy and surrounded by bushes and shrubs.

'Whoever owns this place likes their seclusion, I think,' Jason said and let go of Carole's hand. 'I'll wait here; you go and get the key and no screaming this time, or I will go and take Rusty with me.'

Carole looked down a little embarrassed, but glad that he had come with her. 'OK. I won't be long.' She turned and made for the gate. It was damp and covered in moss where once green paint had protected the now open grain of the wood.

It gave out a horrid noise as she

pushed it on. It was neither a squeak nor a groan, but in its present dark surroundings it made Carole cringe. An owl hooted, adding to her sense of unease. She approached the bungalow door not daring to look up at the overgrown porch just in case a big hairy spider was about to greet her. Carole stepped on the broken tile outside the front door, when it flew open and a bright light shone out.

'You must be Miss Kirkpatrick. I've been waiting for you. Where on earth is your car?' The bright and chirpy voice came from the slight frame of an old lady. She was small even from Carole's viewpoint, but her slight build seemed in contrast to the strength of character that her speech gave away.

'I drive a small Mini and it couldn't make it down the track, the rain has made it so muddy.' Carole didn't want to comment on the potholes that also would have made it impassable to such a low-lying vehicle.

'Oh, you poor dear. Do you want a

cup of tea before you go back?'

'Thank you for the offer but I had better get on before it starts raining again and it becomes any later.'

The old lady nodded her understanding and then shone the oil lamp she was holding at the edge of the trees where Jason was standing, half hidden. 'What about your gentleman friend?'

Carole tried not to smile. She may be old but she doesn't miss a thing. 'No, I don't think he would. It's been a long day and I think we just need to get settled in.' Carole held out the two fifty pound notes. The old lady took them eagerly and handed over the key.

'It has a meter; you'll need some ten pence pieces. I hope you enjoy your stay. Please leave the key under the old tin bath out the back when you go and ring and tell me when you are going.'

'Right. The old tin bath. No problem. Thank you.' Carole turned to walk down the path and was instantly placed into darkness again as the old lady disappeared. I hope it's not the only bath. Jason shone the torch at the ground for her as she approached him.

'Well did she have a bolt through her neck or vampire teeth?' he said as they started back up the track towards Rusty.

'No. Do you have any ten pence pieces on you?' Carole asked wishing she had thought to ask her on the phone about such things. She had been so excited by events that practicalities had flown out of the window. What about towels and sheets?

'Not on me but I have some in the car, not many though. Why?'

'We'll see if we need more when we get there. The old lady said there was a meter.' Carole was anxious to return to Rusty so quickened her step.

'A meter — for what?' Jason asked as he caught up to Carole. His feet were slipping in the carrier bags and he was obviously finding it very frustrating.

'I'm not sure.' Carole glanced at him as he sighed. 'We'll soon find out.' She tried to sound bright but was taken aback by his expression as Rusty came into view. She soon saw why. His back offside wheel had sunk into the mud.

'Now we call for help.' Jason produced his mobile phone from his pocket and switched it on.

'Don't give up so easily,' Carole said enthusiastically.

'If you think for one minute I'm going to push that and fall flat on my face in the mud you have definitely helped the wrong guy.' His face was set. To Carole he looked just like young Thomas when he didn't want to eat his dinner.

'Nobody has to push him, we just need traction.' Carole looked around at the side of the track.

'Traction?' Jason repeated as he switched off his phone and put it carefully back in his pocket.

'Yes, we're surrounded by it.' She bent down and picked up a broad stick. 'Small broken branches.' Carole laid each branch she found either in front or behind the wheel that was rutted in the mud. She made sure that he had enough to cover the moist ground and get him back on to the firmer ground. Then she went to open the driver's door. It was locked.

'I thought he wasn't worth stealing?' Carole repeated Jason's words.

'He isn't, but my laptop is.' Jason gave Carole the car keys.

'You stand at the side until I get him on the road again.'

Jason nodded agreement and watched as she carefully slipped her wellies off and put them in a plastic bag before starting the small car and releasing him from his rut. Within minutes he was free from the suction of the mud and back on the road.

'Well done. Now can we please get to this warm, welcoming haven of utter peace and rest before I freeze to death or expire from hunger.' Jason shook off the bags and sat in the car.

'You shouldn't litter the countryside,' Carole gently reprimanded him as he tossed the bags aside and slammed Rusty's door.

'Don't lose sleep over it, they'll biodegrade.' He pointed along the road.

Reluctantly she drove away from the litter, as she didn't want to put her wellies back on to retrieve them. They slowly made their way back to the main road but Carole was starting to feel very uneasy. A light splatter of rain came down and she pulled Rusty over to the side of the road again.

'Now what's wrong?' Jason sighed heavily. 'Don't tell me that deep rumbling noise wasn't your stomach but a tyre.'

'I think so. The traction we used must have given it a slow puncture.' Carole pulled out the torch again.

'Are you a member of an auto-recovery scheme?' Jason asked searching again for his mobile.

'What for? All we need to do is put on his spare tyre.' Carole zipped up her coat and pulled her big cagoule off the back seat for Jason.

'We need to do. The traction we used?' Jason stared at her.

'OK. The traction that I used and I do need your help to change the tyre.' Carole reached into the glove compartment and pulled out her old driving gloves. She tried hard not to knock Jason's knees as she did.

'I'm sorry to disappoint you again but I've never changed a wheel in my life.'

'I know what to do but I'll need your muscle to help me. An electric drill-thing fastened on that wheel. I won't be able to release its nuts with my wheel brace without some help. Look on it as part of the adventure. It will take your mind off other problems.' Carole smiled. For a moment he looked at her bemused then laughed.

'You have a novel way of looking at life.' He pulled her old cagoule on and got out of the car.

Carole opened the boot and handed him their bags. 'You best put these on your seat whilst I get out the spare.'

Carole soon had the good tyre lying on the roadside next to the flat one. Next she fetched out the wheel brace and took off the covers that protected the nuts.

In fairness she did try to move them but her strength was not sufficient to produce the leverage needed. Jason did the honourable thing and after a few moments of swearing and groaning the wheel was off.

Carole gave as precise instructions as she could to him, so that they soon had four good tyres on Rusty again. Jason even carried the flat to the back of the car, replacing it into the spare's usual home.

Then he looked down at the mud on his hands, trousers and cagoule sleeves. Colour flooded to his face. Carole quickly reached into the groceries and unwrapped a roll of kitchen towel.

'Here, use this for your hands but don't rub your trousers as it would be easier to get off once it's dried.'

'I can't remember ever being so cold,

wet, dirty and hungry in my life!' He brought the bags from his seat and placed them in the boot. As Carole locked it up he returned to the car throwing her cagoule on to the back seat.

'You're very lucky then.' Carole turned the key and Rusty started first time. She turned up his heating and produced her 'in car stereo' from the pocket of the driver's door. It comprised of an old portable CD player and two tiny speakers approximately an inch and a half square. She balanced these on the dashboard, and selected an easy listening tape to soothe the mood a little.

Jason momentarily distracted by what she was doing, did not answer her immediately. 'How am I lucky? My girlfriend has left me, my play has folded before it even opened — I try to escape from it all to regain some sanity and end up freezing in a tin can, covered with mud! I'm on the way to God knows what, with . . . with . . .'

'Me?' Carole finished his outburst before he could insult her as well as Rusty.

'With Cliff Richard singing *Miss You Nights* in the background!' he finished.

'Like I said, you're lucky you've never been so cold or hungry in your life before. Now we have biscuits, cold sausage rolls, yoghurt or fruit drinks and fruit that we can eat now if you are so desperate. What would you like? The car is full of groceries — so there is no need to starve. The heater is on so you shall be warm and the music can be turned off. As for where we're going, if God really does know, then that's fine by me. So what's your poison?' Carole gestured at the bags of food.

'Why am I tempted to say 'you'?' Jason shook his head as if resigning himself to fate. 'Fruit and a yoghurt drink, please.'

Carole rummaged around until she found them and gave him another piece of kitchen towel to wipe his hands on and a bag for his rubbish.

'Thomas must be well looked after,' Jason laughed. 'A mile from here, take the road on the right to Shoreham; the Retreat's five-hundred yards up on the left, according to these instructions.'

'OK.'

Carole put the music off.

'Do you have any Handel, perhaps?'

'Yes,' Carole grinned. 'On the door.'

9

At ten minutes to midnight on the most unusual day of Carole's life she drove up a steep, wooded bank and took a right turn into a narrow drive. She was both tired and hungry, yet the adrenaline surging around her body kept her alert with the pure excitement of an adventure she would never have conjured up, even in her wildest dreams.

And Carole had always dreamed. It took her mind off the problems that reality had frequently put in her path. Jason sat forwards in his seat. Although Jason had responded to every encounter so far with the air of banality, of one who had already experienced everything life could throw at him, he also seemed to have a degree of anticipation about him. They stared ahead of them for a moment at the timber cabin which was dimly lit by Rusty's somewhat limited headlights.

It appeared to have been painted a pale blue. Either the headlights were not doing it justice, or it needed a new coat of paint. The small single storey cabin looked as though it had had an extra room built on, dormer style, into its roof. The cabin was dark, deserted and had trees growing at either side.

'I hope the front of it has more windows. That is, I sincerely hope, that this is the back,' Jason said dryly. 'Or we are in for a very dark and cosseted stay. At least it has a door.'

'That must be the back door.' Carole observed the old tin bath propped up next to it. The old lady had said to leave the keys under it at the back of the cabin. Crumbs! If this is the back, the front must be facing a solid wall of trees. Some retreat this is.

Carole tried to make her voice sound calm and controlled, as if what she was seeing was no less than she would have expected. Although it was — a lot less.

'The downstairs window will be a kitchen one, I presume. The bedroom windows will be at the front, like the main room,' Carole said optimistically.

'Talking of bedrooms, how many does it have?' Jason asked.

'She said it slept two, so we'll be all right,' Carole answered. She hadn't really given the matter any thought until now. Carole could feel her cheeks flush because she realised Jason was sitting staring straight at her.

'Would that be two people sleeping separately or together?' He raised a sceptical eyebrow at her.

'Separately of course! Do you think this is all some elaborate pick up? I'm not that desperate you know.' Carole tried to sound as dignified and suitably insulted as she could, and hoped like hell he could not sense just how desperate she was, about her life, about William, about her past and her lack of future if she didn't change her present lifestyle.

'You're not that desperate. What is

that supposed to mean?' His colour was rising too.

'What I said. That I'm not desperate enough to pick up any strange man who just happened to be loitering on the end of a pier!' Carole fought her corner feeling very self-righteous and wondering what William would think of her now — if he knew where she was, which of course he didn't. Nobody except Jason did.

'Would you have to be desperate to pick me up, Jason Forbes? Or just paid by the Press to do it! Is there a photographer hiding in the bushes, ready to pounce the minute we alight from the car together, making tomorrow's headlines instantly?'

'Who'd believe me if I told them the truth of what really happened?' Jason directed the question to her but he could just as easily have been asking it of himself.

'Ah, then you do believe in me. This is the truth.' Carole gestured to all around them with her hands. 'We were meant to meet on that pier. Somehow we can both help each other. So let's find out how. I'm well aware that I'm not your type, so let's skip any embarrassing moments and agree to settle in there, together, but in separate rooms — OK?' Carole reached for the torch and found the key. She placed them on her lap and held Rusty's steering wheel again.

'Why do you think you're not my type then?' Jason asked as an amused expression spread broadly across his face.

Carole looked at him as he rested against the passenger door. Far from being annoyed he looked completely relaxed, almost happy. 'Because, I'm at least one foot too short, fifteen years beyond your preferred optimum age — five inches too round and not sophisticated enough in my taste in clothes, cars or music.'

'Should I stop there or have I missed something obvious out?' Carole felt perfectly calm as she spoke to him. Her eyes never left his, nor did she shrink at all in stature as she stared back at him.

They were totally incompatible, it was a truth she had to accept, but at least she had been given the opportunity to get to know him — the real Jason Forbes, not the digitally displayed image on a TV screen. Besides, at least she knew who and what she was, which were two things she wondered if he really did. 'Should we go now or have you become attached to my 'Matchbox car'?'

Carole parked Rusty outside the door and stepped out into the unknown. The night air made her shiver as she stood up despite her coat. The air had the faint smell of salt in it. The sea was somewhere out there in the darkness, beyond the trees.

Jason appeared at the other side of Rusty. She shone the torch at the door whilst she placed the key in the lock. It was a little bit stiff initially but it turned allowing her to open the door.

'It didn't creak, that's a good sign,'

Jason whispered into her ear. He had rested his chin on her shoulder. Carole could smell his musk and felt like leaning her face into his. His warmth was comforting; for one moment of self-indulgence she did not want to move.

'Are we going to wait for something to say BOO?' Jason shouted the last word and laughed at his own joke.

She jumped, nearly dropping the torch on the cold stone floor inside the doorway. 'Very funny,' Carole snapped trying to cover up her obvious attack of the jitters. 'You must've been a hoot as a schoolboy.'

Without saying a word he took the torch from her and pushed past her into what was the kitchen. He shone the torch around the plainly painted walls of the small room. Under the window was the old stone enamelled sink. It was deep and oblong in shape. Large taps overhung it. Jason ran the water from both taps.

'Warm and cold running water,' he

grumbled before turning them off again.

'That's promising. If the water heater had not been on I would not have expected hot water in a place like this. We'll have to find the meter soon.' Carole looked around as Jason was shining the torch along the wall next to the door, looking for a light switch. He found it hidden behind an old ironing board and flicked the lights on. A solitary central light bulb lit up the room.

'Can't be more than forty watts.' He took the torch back out to the car and they unloaded the bags on to the kitchen table.

'This is a nice piece of oak.' Jason stopped to admire the old table whilst Carole locked up Rusty then unpacked their provisions into what cupboard space she could find. This was a double cupboard, which had originally been painted with white gloss. It had obviously been repainted many times, but judging by the creamy hue to its current cover, not in the last few years, Carole thought. An old fridge buzzed away merrily in the corner of the room.

'At least this still works,' Carole said, as she loaded it up with milk and other perishables.

'Let's have a hot drink,' Jason said as he faced the cooker with a look of horror. It was obviously old by the number of chips in its once gleaming cream enamel. 'It's gas!'

'I wonder. Do you think it's safe?' Carole asked doubtfully as she looked at it. She had a fear of things that could explode, like Calor gas picnic stoves and fires.

'There's only one way to find out. I don't suppose you smoke, do you?' Jason asked as he ferreted through the three kitchen drawers.

'Nope, but I brought some candles,' Carole answered as she put the last tin in a cupboard.

'Was I supposed to follow the logic of that last statement?' Jason had his head in the cupboard under the sink.

'No, I don't smoke, but I do have matches because I brought some candles.' Carole turned to face him as he stood up. He produced some matches from the cupboard.

'Good, because I can't abide a smoke-filled room.' He grinned then turned on the gas. 'Stand back!' he shouted and Carole backed off to the other side of the room. He lit the gas ring and laughed at her. 'You're very gullible, aren't you?'

'Tea or coffee?' Carole chose to ignore him as the light flickered above her. 'I think we had better find the meter, or we may need the candles.' She picked up the torch and went along a narrow corridor, which was about four feet long. It was panelled in artificial wood that had a cupboard door on the left-hand side. Carole opened it to find the meter, which clearly showed the needle just touching the empty mark. 'Jason I think you'd better . . . '

'Blast!' The exclamation came from the kitchen as the cabin plunged into darkness and the light flickered and died out.

'Jason, I think you'd better locate the ten pence pieces. The meter's empty.' Carole was standing in the doorway to the kitchen watching Jason who was himself standing and shaking his hand in the air.

The flame of the gas ring cast a glow over him, which made him look surreal. How appropriate. Jason grabbed an old towel from the back of a chair and carefully wrapped it around the handle of the kettle. He carefully picked up the old metal kettle again and put it back down on the ring.

'That thing nearly took my skin off. It should have a cover on its handle.' The kettle's lid started lifting as the boiling water fought to escape.

He lifted it up to pour the water into two mugs. 'Find those candles, please, and we shall have a light repast before bed.'

Carole did as she was told. Jason lit them and melted some wax on to a pair of saucers and carefully placed a candle in each, holding them firmly until they had set and could stand upright on their own. Then he put them down on the table. Next he placed each mug on a saucer.

He took the cream from the fridge and, with a confident and steady hand, ran it over the back of a spoon on to the top of the mugs of coffee, which had a strong smell of whisky about them. 'Sit down,' he said to Carole as he placed two mini croissants on a plate in front of her. On a side plate were a delicate knob of butter and a spoonful of fruit preserve.

Carole sat and turned off the torch. She couldn't help admiring the proficiency he showed settling into this strange and primitive kitchen. He may be pampered but he was a 'foody'? With any luck he'll like cooking — please? Carole did the basic meals needed for her and Thomas but hated entertaining.

Judy took great delight in having

144

'friends' around for dinner parties. She suddenly felt very tired and hungry. The Gaelic coffee warmed her as it trickled down her throat and the croissants appeased her hunger. 'This is my second Gaelic in one day.'

'No. The other one was a poor imitation, and besides, that was yesterday. It's ten past midnight and I suggest after this we go to bed. Tomorrow we can explore.' Jason handed her a knife. He looked tired, but relaxed.

Carole stared at him in the candlelight, studying every line on his face and marvelling at every contour. Oh Jason, if only!

Jason pulled his mobile phone out of his pocket. He switched it on and instantly it started beeping. He shook his head and started running his fingers through his hair again with his right hand. Carole could see the tension returning.

'How many messages have you been sent?'

'Ten so far. All from my agent.' He

switched it off and put it back in his pocket.

'None from Melissa?' Carole asked innocently.

'You finished?' His question cut across hers. 'I'd like to go to bed.'

'Yes I have. It was lovely. Let's find out where they are.' Carole blew out the candles after switching on her torch again.

'I'll dig out the ten pences tomorrow. We need to be sparing on the electricity until we find a plentiful supply of them.'

Once again he took the torch from her and led the way. The narrow corridor led them to one wide room that took up much of the front of the cabin. The wooden panelled walls were racked with books from floor to ceiling, and a large window, stretched across the front of the room.

Heavy curtains were pulled across it resting on a long window seat. Opposite, a low soft leather settee took pride of place. It had been well worn but looked comfortable — ideal for curling up and reading a good book in.

Carole realised she was standing next to a door on her right. She opened it to find a shower room and toilet. 'Oh that's a relief. Jason, I need the torch a minute.' She took it from him and locked the door behind her. The whisky in her coffee had made her feel light-headed but the biting cold of this room brought her senses back to her.

It was completely tiled. The floor tiles were a terracotta colour whilst the walls were covered in small white tiles. With no visible heater, it was freezing. Not a room to hang about in.

When she re-emerged Jason said, 'Thanks, my turn.' He took the torch and Carole was left in the darkness. She edged further along the wall and banged her head on something metal.

Jason soon rejoined her, shivering as he walked past and climbed up what she could now see was an iron spiral staircase. She followed him and they both were delighted to see that the

147

bedroom overlooked the treetops on the bank, giving a clear view out to sea. By the moonlight they could see the white light as it highlighted each gentle wave. Even the stars were shining brightly.

'It's marvellous,' Carole remarked as she admired the view.

'Yes it is, but I don't know where yours is?'

Carole looked at Jason not understanding what he meant until she saw him looking at the bed behind them. It had been built into a wooden surround. The headboard had a carved ship's wheel in the centre of it. A rope design edged it, and the bed, which Carole estimated, was made of a five-foot mattress, filled most of the room. A one-foot surround provided a seat, but was actually the top of a base cupboard that contoured the bed.

Jason took off his shoes and climbed in fully clothed.

'I can't sleep downstairs!' Carole said, horrified at the thought. It was cold, dark and she didn't know if there was any extra bedding.

'Then sleep up here,' Jason said, as he lay there, fully clothed, with his eyes closed, huddling the duvet around him.

I must be mad. Females would throw themselves at him, yet I . . . I can't. What about William? What would he think? Carole shivered and kicked off her shoes. She climbed into the other side of the bed.

'Wise decision. Don't worry, your virtue is safe, pretty maiden,' Jason drawled as he yawned.

'Yes, I know, I'm not your type. We've been through that already. OK?' Carole answered, as she wrapped herself up in the duvet, and felt the warmth enveloping her.

Within ten minutes he started to snore.

10

William was ill at ease. The evening had been fun but had ended with a badly handled rejection. Sue had come to him, sure that she could start up where they had left off. She wanted him to go with her now. Even her offer did not tempt him, he had changed so much. He did not want to hurt her, but she had left early anyway deciding not to waste more time on a lost cause as she put it.

He was surprised to feel relief. Listening to Carole's voice on the answer phone, he felt uneasy. Again, he had been distracted by Sue, and had never had the opportunity to speak to Carole on her own. He had so wanted to. It was something he needed to know about them, was he imagining a friendship that was something more or less than what he hoped it would be.

After having Sue's enforced attentions he decided it was time he talked to Carole. The voice said she had gone away but not where. Strange, he thought.

He knew where her sister's house was and decided that he would make enquiries as to when she was coming back. It was a worryingly vague message. He then remembered that she had wanted to speak to him before the meeting and then during it, had not become involved in any of the planning or events.

He pulled on his jacket. Something must have happened and she had been trying to talk to him but his thoughts had been elsewhere — on Sue.

He picked up his car keys and wallet and decided to try and unravel a mystery and help a friend — a very special and dear friend, only he had not had the courage to tell her just how much of one she was.

★ ★ ★

151

Carole opened her eyes to a strange world. The air was cooler and fresher than her normal centrally heated room in Maple Drive. She gazed out of the large low double glazed window opposite the bed where she was lying, fully clothed.

Carole sat up and huddled the duvet to her as she marvelled at the view. She could see over the treetops, as the bank descended to the coast road, and out to the sea beyond. It was as if the world was laid out before her just waiting for her to explore it.

Then she looked at the empty bed beside her, and thought about Jason. She touched the space where he had slept — it was cold. Had he left already? Did he get a fright when he woke up and, in the light of day, wondered what madness had brought him there?

Carole stood up, grabbed her toilet bag and ran down the spiral staircase. The room that greeted her was quite different to how she had imagined it in the dim light of her old torch. The

152

wooden bookshelves were dark; however, the light from the large window brought out all the colours of the clip mat and the tapestry throw, which covered the faded deep red leather settee.

Despite her curiosity over the whereabouts of Jason, Carole stopped for a moment and admired the Thai elephants carved out of hardwood that stood proudly on a low-tiled coffee table and the Batik orchid print that was displayed on the wall above the settee. They were noticeably different to the more expected artefacts such as the ship in a bottle, the brass barometer and a mounted dead fish of some sort.

Carole sniffed the air. A pleasantly sweet and pleasant aroma was drifting her way from the kitchen. She walked along the short corridor and cautiously looked around the door. She half expected to see the old lady there with her apron on. A bizarre idea perhaps, but then she could hardly have expected that Jason would be standing by the cooker expertly controlling the gas ring to make what she considered perfect pancakes. Perhaps just a little bit thin.

'I heard you get up. Breakfast will be ready in five minutes, make sure you are.' Jason gave out the order without looking around. Such confidence.

Carole ran to the bathroom. It felt like minus ten in there so she had no trouble being at the table within three minutes.

Jason produced two warmed plates from the small oven and then served breakfast.

'Wow! These look great. I've never had pancakes for breakfast before.' Carole's eyes were glued to the pan, where the pancakes had been delicately folded into quarters and were covered in a hot orange sauce. The pan stopped momentarily.

'They are crepes — almond crepes served with fresh orange in an orange sauce.' He continued to serve them; using tongs he lifted each one out until

154

a neat row of four folded crepes rested against each other on her plate. Carefully he drizzled the orange sauce over them and then arranged orange slices neatly along the side. Next, a cup of what Carole called 'proper' coffee was placed at the side and a jug of warm milk in front of her.

'Well?' Jason sat down opposite her, arms folded casually as he slouched back in the chair. 'Are you going to let them go cold or eat them?'

'Eat them.' Carole wasted no time; she savoured every delicate mouthful. The orange sauce was spiked with something. She decided it must have been the Grand Marnier she had bought for him in the supermarket.

'Thanks for doing breakfast, Jason. I'll do tomorrow's.' Carole offered.

'No thanks,' Jason chuckled to himself. 'You can do the washing up.'

After Carole had finished, she washed up as promised and Jason drifted into the living room. Carole zipped up her fleece and joined him. He had changed trousers and wore a thick cable knit jumper.

Everything about him seemed to spell *money*. His watch was not a normal watch; his hair was cut so, no matter how many times he ruffled it, it always fell back into its layered style. Carole laughed to herself, even with a simple bob she always seemed to look as though she had come through the proverbial hedge backwards.

'What would you like to do today?' Carole asked him as he stared out of the window. The lawn fell away to the bank and the trees that last night seemed to surround the cottage, tapered away from each side as a natural boundary to the lawn, before descending the bank.

'I want to relax,' he said, without taking his hands from his pockets. 'So what do you suggest we do?' He turned his head, and peered down towards her. For a brief moment she thought his eyes drifted from her to the spiral staircase, which led to the bedroom.

'Let's go for a walk and explore,'

Carole said enthusiastically.

'It's been raining. The ground is all wet. That would not be relaxing,' Jason grumbled and his gaze returned to the view from the window.

'Yes, it would. Let yourself go a bit. Think back to younger days, your childhood. Have some fun!' Carole smiled as he ran his hand through his hair and looked back down at her. Delicious — like his panc . . . crepes.

'When I was a child I didn't care what state my shoes got into. Now, as I have only one pair with me, I do.' He sat down on the old sofa and pulled his mobile phone out of his trouser pocket.

'I know . . . ' Carole started to say.

'Somehow, I thought you would, but scream all you like I will not wear carrier bags again!' He pressed the button on the phone and instantly it started beeping as messages reached their destination.

'The old lady said that there was a village a few miles farther on. She said that we could buy anything we need there.' Carole watched his face crease in annoyance at whatever he was reading on the phone.

'I'm sure you could find everything you need there, but I doubt I would.' Although he answered her he continued to read his messages.

'Yes — you would!' Carole was surprised by her own schoolmarmish tones as much as Jason was. He actually peeled his focus from his phone and looked straight at her. He is not used to being openly challenged.

'I'm certain you would find everything you need for your basic survival, but not necessarily everything you would want for your creature comforts.' She folded her arms and looked down upon this grown man, who had adopted the air of a sulky child.

His messages obviously had not pleased him.

'So what do I need, oh wise one?' His voice was harsh and mocking.

'Welly boots, of course.' Carole smiled. 'Then we can go for a walk and get wet. Oh, and a waterproof. Switch it off and put it in a drawer somewhere until you've had a chance to unwind.' Carole laughed at the look of horror that swept across his face when she used the word 'off.'

'I can't.'

'Yes you can. Just press the little button and give it to me. I'll put it where you won't find it. Then if you're tempted to switch on again, you can't.'

'Impossible. How would I know what was happening? How would they reach me?' Jason sounded appalled by the idea.

'But you ran away so they could not find you.' Carole took a step back as he turned abruptly to face her, pointing his index finger at her.

'I did not run away! I am no coward. I stand and face my problems.'

He was almost shouting at her. Instead of being frightened she admired the power of the man. She had seen her hero react like that when challenging the authority of the admiralty.

'Perhaps there is a time to stand and

a time to take a break. You have chosen to have a break. Put the phone off. Disconnect yourself from the rat-race and allow yourself time again.'

'I haven't time to myself have I?' Jason stared directly at her.

Carole was taken aback. She felt the colour rise in her cheeks. 'I can soon remedy that.' Carole ran upstairs and packed her few things into her bag. She felt like crying, screaming that life was unfair and she had been a fool when she heard his footsteps behind her. Before she could turn around she smelt his musk and felt his hands firmly but gently rest on her shoulders.

He kissed her gently and whispered softly, 'I'm sorry. That was unforgivable of me. Please stay and forgive my outburst.'

Forgiven, heaven . . . it's so easy for him.

Carole cleared her throat and dropped the bag and moved away from the bed. Stupid girl. Why can't it be as simple as the movies?

'So we go to the shops then?' Carole asked as she pulled Rusty's keys from her pocket.

'Yes,' he sighed, 'we go to the shops.' He put the mobile phone in the bedside drawer and shut it firmly.

'Good. I'm glad you have decided to relax,' Carole said as she half skipped down the stairs.

'When will you?' he asked, as they walked to the car.

'I am already,' Carole answered with a broad smile as she opened Rusty's door and climbed in.

'You're running as much as I,' he replied as he placed the small cassette player on Rusty's dashboard and looked at the very limited supply of music.

'No, I'm not. I just need a bit of space to put a few things into perspective, that's all,' Carole explained as she reversed Rusty back out on to the road.

'Exactly what I mean.' Jason chuckled. 'You've lost it, haven't you? You're scared.'

'What are you talking about?' Carole tried to sound calm and confident. She was here helping him. She didn't need him prying into her problems. They were trivial matters compared with theatre productions and broken engagements.

'Admit it. You've run into a wall and don't know how to get around or over it. What's the story with this William?' He was grinning at her as she drove.

'William is the curate. I told you.' Carole changed gear and crashed it making a horrible grating sound. Jason openly laughed.

'OK. OK. I'll mind my own business or else Matchbox will need a new elastic band.'

They drove into a small market town and found a place to park outside a warehouse shop. It obviously catered for a lot of agricultural supplies for the local farmers.

'We'll get your boots and waterproof here. Do you have any cash left?'

'Yes, what do you want?' Jason

produced his wallet.

'I don't want anything from that, but if you have cash then your name won't blaze out as it would from a credit card,' Carole said sharply, still flustered over his questioning about William.

He seemed to have found a way to unnerve her. She didn't quite know how to regain her composure whilst under his constant stare. He's toying with me. Get a grip, girl, or you're going to make a fool of yourself.

'You sure you don't want anything from me?' Jason was holding his wallet in his hand.

'Quite sure!' Carole slammed Rusty's door firmly behind her as she got out. She heard him laugh. She gritted her teeth and forced a smile as he shut Rusty's other door with almost exaggerated care.

11

The day was cool but dry. William phoned Judy on his mobile. 'Hello, this is William. I wondered if I could speak to Carole?' He knew he sounded nervous.

'Oh, is it? You the one from the church?' The voice of her sister was the opposite of the warmth of Carole's own.

'Yes, that's right. She may have mentioned me.'

'You're right there! So what did you say to her to make her run away? Did you turn her down flat?'

The anger surprised him.

'I told her she was having some sort of stupid crush thing but she wouldn't hear it. Now you made her go away. Fine man of God you are. So where is she? How am I supposed to cope with Tom full time at short notice? If you hear from her, tell her to contact me, or better still, come home.' The phone went dead.

William stared at it. 'Carole felt the same way about him and he had dared not say anything to her because . . . because . . . he was a fool — a fool for God and with it came vulnerability and responsibility. But he had hurt the most precious person to him and that he would never ever have wanted to do. If Judy did not know where Carole had gone, then where would he find her?'

He did not know, but he made his way back to the church and thought back over the last few days. His bike had been borrowed and returned. Suddenly he felt that this was the only thing he could think of that was strange.

He decided to return to the hall. The bike was still there. He looked at the notice board and rearranged some of them. Removing a few out of date ones, it was then he saw the space. What had been there? The cabin!

He ran into the vicarage and looked at the old telephone book. There it was, The Captain's Retreat. He phoned the number.

'Excuse me, I am the Curate at St Bedes. I am enquiring as to the whereabouts of my friend, Carole Kirkpatrick. I believe she has rented a cottage from you,' he asked the lady.

'Yes, that's correct. Mind, it was near midnight when they arrived. Poor thing was wet through.' The voice sounded concerned.

'How long has she booked it for?' he asked, expecting to be told to mind his own business.

'Oh, they've got it for a week.'

'They? Sorry, I presumed she was alone.'

'No, she had a man friend with her, but he stood back. I didn't see him proper as he let her do all the talking and give me the two notes.' The woman was telling him more than she should and William realised that she was concerned about them.

'Sorry, what notes?' he asked, his mind racing to make sense of this.

'Fifty pound notes. I hope they are real as I've not seen one before now.'

'Thank you,' he said and rang off. This was worrying. Carole didn't use fifties and who was the man?

With more than a little concern he packed a small case, phoned Arthur's wife, made his apologies to the wardens and dismissed himself on personal problems for a day or two as he drove down the coast. If Carole had got herself into some sort of trouble she would need help. If not, then he would indeed look and feel a fool, but his conscience would be clear.

Carole went for a walk around the village shops. She stopped to buy a paper. On page five, in a small corner, it ran a piece on Jason Forbes. It reported that his new play was in crisis as a dispute between the backers had posed a severe threat to it opening on time.

Mr Forbes' agent was quoted as saying that Jason, on doctor's advice, had taken a short break after contracting a flu virus. The article finished on an optimistic note, that the play could still open on time, if the current dispute was quickly resolved.

Carole bought the paper then walked over to the post office and general store. As she did, Jason appeared from the chemist's shop.

'Been buying your flu relief tablets?' Carole asked, to be greeted by a broad grin.

'Not exactly,' he said. 'Are you expecting us to succumb?'

Carole showed him the article. He shrugged his shoulders. 'They'll cover for me for a week then I'll have to go back.' He held up a big carrier, which carried the logo of *Southern Valley Farmers*. 'I am the proud owner of a Berghaus all-weather coat and Wellington boots. So I shan't freeze or get wet again, even if we climb mountains! It shall grieve me sorely to part with your cagoule, but I feel I must.' He handed her a smaller bag that was obviously heavier than it should be if her waterproof were the only thing inside.

She peeped in the bag to see another all-weather coat. Fleece included.

'Close your mouth, Carole, or you'll catch flies.' Jason did not wait for her to say anything; he just turned and walked towards the car.

'You can't! It's over a hundred pounds. I couldn't repay you. It wouldn't be right.' Carole ran alongside him. After regaining her composure from her previous indignation she was completely lost again. It was a beautifully practical present and good quality, but she hardly knew him.

'I can. I have. I don't want repayment. It's a gift. A thank you, for taking me under your wing and away from the rat pack. OK?'

'If you're sure,' Carole said, not knowing if she should — but she loved the coat and was desperately in need of a new one.

'Anyway, your William would approve.' Jason smiled at her.

'Why?' Carole asked.

'Because Christians preach giving, don't they?'

'Yes, selfless giving, I suppose. Thank you for the coat. It's very nice. I accept it as a gift from a friend.' She could not look straight at him, so continued to walk.

'Not from an admirer?' he teased.

'No!' Carole said firmly.

'But I do admire you.' His voice had lost its mocking quality. Carole found that more disturbing. Was he being serious or still mocking her?

Carole looked at him sternly. 'OK. You've taunted me long enough. Let's get back to a more sane footing again, please?'

'I'm serious, Carole. You have to be one of the most straightforward and honest people I've ever met.'

He put his arm around her shoulder as they walked back to Rusty, and Carole felt pangs of guilt because she hadn't been honest with him.

She knew who he was, and was

tempted to wrap her arms around him and respond to the growing feelings that she felt within her whenever he touched her.

I want to be loved, though — a real love. The kind that lasts longer than a week.

* * *

They walked for two hours in the sun, upon moist grass. Once they had stopped at the rise and looked at the view over the country around them, she looked at him.

'Jason, I know who you are. I always have. Your image coloured my childhood as your presence does now. I lied to you.'

He didn't look at her but stared at the view. 'I know.'

'How did you know?' Carole asked, disappointed that he had not believed her.

'Because a lady like yourself would not have adopted a stranger so readily.

You acted as a friend, and I did not wish to discuss the duty of a good Christian here. You acted like a friend and within a safe boundary. Otherwise, you would have taken me to your good friend, Wills, to hide and help.'

He looked at her and winked. 'Still, don't worry, I thought you were playing games with me for a different reason, but then you proved me wrong. You are genuinely a good person, with values that I had thought died out years since. Your Wills is a lucky man.'

'No he isn't because he is not my Wills, his ex has returned and she is beautiful and fun.'

'Then he does not deserve you.'

Carole laughed and looked back at the Retreat. 'I'm starved,' she said.

He held out his hand and she took hold of it as they walked back down. All of those questions that she had longed to ask about her childhood hero came flooding out. By the time they had reached the hut, he was stripped of all the nostalgia and she had learned something of the actual man. He was arrogant, charming, totally self-centred and about to be reunited with his play and girlfriend as his petulant and sudden disappearance had served its purpose.

'You want to go then?' she asked as they walked up to the cottage.

'I have two contracts, you see. Also Melissa is heartily sorry and I need to offer her comfort and understanding.' He winked.

'Why don't you stay here, think about things. I'll leave you my mobile number and you can let me know if you want a place to hide. I've plenty of them where William would never find you or that harridan of a sister of yours.'

He squeezed her hand. 'Thank you,' she answered.

The sound of another car manoeuvring up the lane broke the moment and Carole let go of his hand as a familiar vehicle came into sight. It stopped and out stepped William who was looking anxiously from Carole to

Jason as he approached.

'William!' she exclaimed.

'I'm going to pack. My car will be here at three.' He winked at her and walked into the cottage.

'Carole, I was worried. I didn't realise that you had a . . . I mean I was rude to you the other night, you wanted to talk and there wasn't time.' William was staring at the back of Jason as he disappeared from view.

'Is Sue with you?' Carole asked, trying to stay calm.

'No.' William shook his head. 'It was a mistake her coming. We've changed . . . I've changed. Carole, who is he?' William was obviously really concerned.

'Someone who needed some time to think and I knew the Retreat was empty. It seemed like the perfect place. Will you come and meet him? He's leaving soon.'

William looked at her and placed his hands on both of her shoulders, bringing her in to him. She willingly fell into his arms. Here no-one was watching them, judging them or interfering. Here they had peace. 'I love you, Carole, but if this is my folly, I shall move on. I will not embarrass you and . . . '

She kissed him, an embrace filled with love and warmth and commitment that felt genuine, not a crush, not make believe but real love.

'Stay, we stay, until we both move on.' She saw his lovely smile fill his face and he swung her round full circle.

Jason shouted over to them as her feet touched the ground, 'Coffee anyone?'

'Lovely,' Carole replied and walked arm in arm with William to the lovely aroma.

'Who is he?' William asked again.

'Well, he was my hero, but not any more.' She winked at a bemused William as she led him inside.

We do hope that you have enjoyed reading this large print book.

Did you know that all of our titles are available for purchase?

We publish a wide range of high quality large print books including:
Romances, Mysteries, Classics
General Fiction
Non Fiction and Westerns

Special interest titles available in large print are:
The Little Oxford Dictionary
Music Book, Song Book
Hymn Book, Service Book

Also available from us courtesy of Oxford University Press:
Young Readers' Dictionary
(large print edition)
Young Readers' Thesaurus
(large print edition)

For further information or a free brochure, please contact us at:
Ulverscroft Large Print Books Ltd.,
The Green, Bradgate Road, Anstey,
Leicester, LE7 7FU, England.
Tel: (00 44) **0116 236 4325**
Fax: (00 44) **0116 234 0205**

Other titles in the
Linford Romance Library:

AN IMAGE OF YOU

Liz Fielding

Millionaire Sir Charles Bainbridge, at the end of his patience with his daughter Georgette's behaviour, sends her to Kenya. Humiliatingly, she must work as an assistant to the ultimate male chauvinist Lukas on a location shoot. They met once before . . . in rather strained circumstances! In fact, she'd showered him with flour and he hadn't been pleased. And now she must be nice to him. This will take every ounce of acting ability Georgette possesses — and she is no actress.

TO LOVE AGAIN

Jasmina Svenne

After a disastrous romance in her youth, Juliet Radley has given up hope of marriage and become reconciled to a quiet life as Amy Gibson's governess. However, despite her expectations, she grows attached to Captain Richard Gibson, her employer's cousin — the only house guest to treat her with consideration. But a new arrival threatens her happiness: the rakish Hugh Faversham is the one man in the world who can expose her darkest secret . . .